THE CAPTAIN'S COLLIE

By Ace Mask

Copyright © 2021 Ace Mask
All rights reserved.
ISBN: 1-0879-0874-4
ISBN-13: 978-1-0879-0874-8

Copy Editor: Rose Hutches

Cover Art: Cindy Alvarado
etsy.com/shop/pawprintsportfolio

https://www.facebook.com/colliesofheathercircle

Dedication

To Mark Thomas Mcgee,
my friend for over 58 years

CHAPTER ONE

With its mission nearly complete, the crew of the German bomber flying through the night sky above the chaos and destruction they had rained down upon the city of Coventry prepared to drop their last explosive. With anti-aircraft artillery exploding perilously close on all sides of the plane, the bomb aimer quickly aligned what was left of his final target within his sight. A symbolic red cross on the roof of the hospital below should have marked the building as a haven of safety, but instead only served as an easy target for the enemy, leaving it with nine direct hits during two consecutive nights of attack. On that final night of the latest round of bombings, April 8, 1941, the German aircraft delivered one more catastrophic blow. Within moments, the shell struck the very heart of its objective, with a tumultuous explosion of fire and carnage.

The three crew members and one observer aboard breathed a sigh of relief as the pilot guided their plane away from the city, following the lead of the 230 other Luftwaffe bombers headed back toward their base in France. The men felt a sense of consolation, not because they had any remorse about the many hundreds of civilian deaths and casualties they had caused, for they had long ago numbed themselves of such guilt, but because they now felt safe from the constant barrage of artillery fire to which they had been subjected.

The gunners aboard, one sitting near the pilot in the cockpit and a second in the rear of the plane, remained vigilant as the pilot endeavored to close the gap between his aircraft and the rest of the bombers behind which he was trailing. He had inadvertently separated himself from the others during the mission and failed to rejoin them as promptly as he might have. There was relative safety in numbers, and the pilot was not comfortable with the distance he found himself lagging behind. The crew soon marked the danger they were now courting and their apprehension returned. A strong electric storm was gathering on the horizon, and the flashes of lightning radiating from the clouds did little to calm their nerves.

For a bomber, the Dornier D17 they were flying had a good reputation for speed and dexterity, but the pilot was wary of testing those abilities against a British fighter aircraft, and in his present predicament, he knew well that he was exposed and vulnerable. He tried to gain on the cluster of planes ahead, but they were traveling at the same top speed as he, leaving him and his crew trailing a dangerous distance behind.

Soon the pilot's fears were realised as a single British night fighter aircraft rose into the space between his bomber and the cluster of planes ahead. The fighter immediately directed fire at the German cockpit, and the bomber pilot quickly turned his plane into an ascent, exposing its belly to a steady stream of gunfire that pierced its structure as he attempted to climb up and over the British plane.

The gunner in the tail of the bomber attempted to return fire, but his plane's position made an accurate shot at the attacking plane nearly impossible as it passed beneath before looping around in pursuit. With the bombardier and the observer holding tight, the German pilot leveled his aircraft in an attempt to outrun the fighter, but the British pilot came in low behind, delivering damage to the undercarriage and wings as the bomber's gunner returned fire without success.

The bombardier moved to man a gun mounted on the right side of the craft but was struck in the head by a bullet, knocking him to the floor. Jumping to his feet, the gunner in the rearward position rushed toward the side-mounted gun, but in his eagerness, stumbled over the body of the dead crew member. The observer, who had been making notations in a small notebook during the mission, hastily shoved his notes into his pocket and tossed the body out of the way. The gunner clumsily reached the gun and began firing wildly as he attempted to organize himself. The British fighter dropped to a position directly beneath the German plane, and all exchange of gunfire momentarily ceased.

For what seemed like an eternity, the two aircraft flew in exact parallel positions, one beneath the other, as the Germans nervously waited for the fighter to rise and resume its assault. The gunner yelled at the observer to get behind a second gun mounted on the left side of the aircraft. Though the observer was an officer of much higher rank with no combat flight experience, he promptly obeyed and positioned himself behind the side gun. Removing his gloves and quickly locating the weapon's trigger, he calmly prepared and waited for a target to come into view. After an unsettling minute of inactivity, the British plane suddenly rose on the left side of the bomber and began firing, its bullets striking dangerously close to the observer who calmly took careful aim at the fighter cockpit and returned fire. The German officer's shots were precise, striking the cockpit of his enemy, who reacted by turning his plane away as he dove into the distance. The officer could not clearly determine the damage he had inflicted, and he strained to see if the British plane had gone into a nosedive, but the German plane was now in the midst of ever-thickening clouds, severely limiting visibility.

Believing the British fighter was no longer a threat, the bomber pilot began to take stock of his situation and called out to his crew through the intercom. The surviving gunner reported the loss of the crew member and that the plane had taken heavy gunfire, but nothing he could see indicated that there was any critical damage.

The gunner's report was interrupted by a bolt of lightning that struck the aircraft's left propeller, located on the wing just outside the cockpit. The body of the plane shook fiercely, and the engine sputtered, but the prop continued to spin radically, emitting intermittent flames.

The right engine continued to operate, but the damage made an emergency landing inevitable. The pilot had not yet had time to take stock of his present location, though he knew that in his effort to evade the British fighter he had been thrown way off course and was likely miles away from the body of the fleet he had been trailing.

Lightning continued to strike alarmingly close as the fury of the thunderstorm grew more savage, and the pilot fought for control of the damaged bomber, attempting to drop below the clouds to determine if a landing would be possible. As he labored to lower the plane, however, the right engine began to sputter. He quickly examined his instruments to determine the reason.

The cause was immediately apparent. The aircraft had run out of fuel. How could that be, he wondered. The plane was equipped with self-sealing fuel tanks to protect fuel stored in the wings and fuselage. He reasoned that somehow the main line that delivered fuel to the right engine had been damaged in the fight. This left the pilot with two options: attempt to glide the wounded aircraft to a hazardous landing or order the crew to bail out before crashing. However, as he finally cleared the storm clouds, he promptly recognized that neither option was viable.

Lightning strikes sporadically illuminated a forest reaching upward at a distance far too close and rising far too fast to make a parachute jump feasible. The area was much too thickly wooded to make any safe landing possible. The pilot attempted to lift the plane, hoping in vain that he could glide it to a clearing, but the left propeller continued to spin radically, pulling against his attempt to achieve any kind of control.

Moments later the plane delivered its crew to a deadly crash within the forest, the din of its impact unheard amid the far more deafening sound of thunder.

CHAPTER TWO

Feeling at ease, Doctor Alfred Finlay relaxed behind the wheel of his sedan as he travelled rural England along a little country road that wound through picturesque scenery of gentle fields and rolling grasslands. His soul was comforted by the simple beauty and tranquilizing effect of sheep leisurely grazing upon the landscape, and he smiled and breathed a soothing sigh of pleasure at the therapeutic effect the drive was having on him after having endured five months of unimaginable bedlam. The 65-year-old doctor had lived and served the people of the area for most of his life, and though this visit would be only a quick one, he looked forward to returning home permanently and prayed it would be sometime very soon.

"You're going to enjoy it out here, Alice," he said with a smile to the 11-year-old-girl in the warm duffel coat and blue scarf sitting next to him. "I promise you. Have you ever spent any time in the country?"

"No, sir," the girl said. She had been mostly silent since she and the doctor had begun their drive early that morning, answering questions politely but simply. Her subdued attitude did not go unnoticed, but the older man understood the emotional upset troubling the youngster and refrained from excessive small talk.

Doctor Finlay removed his eyeglasses and handed them to Alice.

"Give these a clean, will you, my dear?" he asked. "I believe you'll find a cloth there in the glove compartment."

Alice complied, giving the glasses a vigorous but careful rub before returning the cloth and handing them back.

"Ah, good," the doctor said. "Now, do me another favor and hold the wheel a moment. Can you do that?"

Hesitantly, Alice leaned toward the wheel and grabbed it with both hands, doing her best to keep the car steady as the doctor used both his hands to place the shell-frame glasses back on. He seemed in no hurry to retake the wheel as he made sure they were comfortably positioned.

"Thank you, Alice," he said when he took control again.

Sizing up the thin, blonde-haired girl in the seat next to him, the doctor was hopeful his decision to temporarily relocate her to the country, away from the havoc and dreadful tragedy she had endured in Coventry during the last few months, would be the best medicine he could prescribe. The comfortable sensations he was feeling that afternoon, as he smoothly navigated the road, convinced him he was doing the right thing for the girl.

Alice, however, seemed oblivious to the beauty outside the car window.

By late afternoon, they arrived at their destination. Entering through a majestic iron gate, the doctor guided his car along a narrow, loose-gravel road that led past majestic trees and well-tended landscape, which soon opened onto an immaculately manicured lawn. Circling around the grassplot, the road delivered the doctor and his passenger before the large manor house that dominated the estate.

The 17th century Tudor style, three-storied building included among its accommodations 10 bedrooms and 7 reception rooms and included an adjacent coach house, stable and various other outbuildings behind which stretched a heavily wooded forest. Despite its age, the house was well maintained and imposing. Alice had never seen anything quite like it in the densely populated area of the city in which she had grown up, and her attention was at last diverted.

The doctor's demeanor unexpectedly turned quite serious as he turned off the engine and positioned himself to face her.

"This is the home of Captain Bramwell," he said. "He doesn't live in the main house, so you likely won't see much of him. He's taken up residence in a cottage in the back. He prefers to keep to himself, but if you should encounter him, I must advise you to avoid him. I'm telling you this for your own good. I'm certain you'll be comfortable here, so long as you heed my warning and stay away from Captain Bramwell. Do you understand?"

Alice nodded quickly. Throughout their drive, the doctor had been cheerful and pleasant, but his warning and the seriousness with which the words were spoken made her uneasy. Where she had been indifferent about her relocation, she was now filled with gloom and reluctance.

The doctor regretted having to deliver his caution with such earnestness, but he knew it was important to make a strong impression on the girl. Relaxing, he smiled and patted her on the shoulder.

"Now, let's investigate your new lodgings, shall we?"

From the back seat, Doctor Finlay lifted the girl's small, worn suitcase and the gas mask strapped to it and handed it to her before they walked to the front door. The doctor pushed the buzzer.

Awaiting a response, Alice was struck with the silence in the air, only punctuated with the soothing sound of a few chirping birds in the trees nearby. Having grown up amid the constant sounds of a bustling, industrialized city she was unaccustomed to such quiet, and for the moment, as she surveyed the grounds in front of the house, the apprehension the doctor's words had cast was pushed aside.

Suddenly the stillness was broken by the sound of a barking dog. Alice craned her neck to identify the source of the sound, which was coming from an area at the side of the house. It was there, standing at the edge of a dirt pathway that led through a cluster of trees to the back of the residence, that she saw a large, magnificent collie. Alice had never owned a dog herself, and most of those she encountered on the streets outside her home apartment were mixed-breeds, mostly strays, who begged for scraps and scavenged the garbage cans for food. Since the bombing had begun, there were many strays, and many were killed, some at the hand of their owners who thought to spare them from injury caused by falling bombs. She had never seen a dog like the one who stood in the distance, steadily barking and wagging his tail. She understood that it wasn't a warning bark, though. It was a greeting.

There, amid the rays of the setting sun, his broad, snowy white chest and thick, mahogany coat were the embodiment of dignity and bearing. The dog's ears, which stood tall and proud on his head, were tipped slightly and even from that distance, Alice could make out what seemed to her to be a cheery expression on his long, soft, pointed muzzle.

As quickly as it had begun, the dog stopped barking as the two of them made eye contact. The collie sat, his tail still wagging as it brushed aside the dust of the pathway, and his head tilted slightly, as if he were questioning why Alice was there.

Doctor Finlay took no notice of the dog, and soon the door was answered by a thin, balding, uniformed butler who greeted him by name with an air of formality. Stepping aside, he admitted the two visitors, who were ushered into the entryway, where the Doctor handed him his hat and topcoat before they were asked to wait.

Alice stood in awe as she regarded the house's grand, impressive furnishings, all heirlooms that might have been passed down through many generations, though carefully polished and maintained. She imagined that they had sat in exactly the same spot they were now, perhaps placed there when the old house was first built. The paintings that hung majestically upon the walls were mostly landscapes, alternating with images of various animals, some domestic and others strange and unknown to the girl. A staircase against the wall wound its way to a landing above. Despite the embellishment of a few potted plants, the atmosphere, the seeming age of its appointments along with the silence that engulfed the house, made her feel as if it was an unhappy place. There was no life in it.

"Missus Thorndike will see you in the study, Doctor Finlay," the butler announced as he held open a door that led off from the main entry.

Alice reached for her suitcase, but the doctor held up a hand.

"No, you wait here, Alice," he said. "I won't be a moment."

She watched as the doctor entered the room, and the door was closed behind him. The butler walked aloofly by and receded down a hallway near the staircase, leaving her alone and uneasy in the strange house. She could faintly hear the voice of Doctor Finlay conversing with a lady in the next room, and she hastily rushed to a wooden chair that stood near the door. Sitting down, and by leaning her ear against the wall, she was just barely able to discern their words.

In the next room, a tall, thin, severe-looking woman dressed in black was seated behind a desk in the neatly organized study. A collection of ledgers and papers that lay before her was pushed aside as she stood, removing a pair of steel-rimmed glasses and offering her hand in greeting.

"Good afternoon, Doctor," she said.

"A very good afternoon to you, Missus Thorndike," he said, taking her hand with a formal smile.

The smile was not returned, however, as she gestured to a chair in front of her desk.

"Ridley will return with tea shortly," she informed him as she seated herself.

"So very good of you, ma'am, but I'm afraid I shall have to decline," he said, sitting. "I'm expected back in Coventry by tomorrow morning, so I must be on my way."

"I understand," she acknowledged with a nod. "And how are things there? The reports on the wireless are filled with ghastly stories of destruction and human suffering. Is it all as bad as reported?"

The doctor sighed. "I doubt that the reports you've been hearing could adequately describe it. Perhaps you heard, Christ Church was destroyed a few weeks ago, as well as ... "

He didn't need to finish his report. Mrs. Thorndike was well aware that Coventry-Warwickshire Hospital had been badly damaged.

"What absolute monsters are those people?" she asked with a shake of her head. "Factories, yes, but churches, hospitals, innocent civilians? The devil has a hand in this war, you can be sure of it!"

"The girl's mother," the doctor said, leaning in close and lowering his voice, "worked with me at the hospital. A Missus Piper. Best nurse I've ever known. She was the kindest, most devoted and hard-working .... I came to rely on her tremendously."

"How did she die, Doctor?"

Outside the room, Alice stiffened. She knew better than anyone how it happened.

"Oddly enough, it happened the morning after the bombing had ceased," the doctor related. "Long after the 'all clear' had sounded. You can't imagine the state the hospital was in. Absolute pandemonium. No water, no electricity, glass and debris and collapsed walls and ceilings everywhere. We had moved a number of patients to the basement for safety during the bombing, and I found her in the lobby helping some poor child who had been injured. I ordered her to the basement to assist as best she could."

Alice heard the approach of the butler as he returned with a tea tray. She jumped from the door and pretended to examine a painting on a wall nearby. The butler eyed her suspiciously as he knocked on the door and awaited a response. He entered the room and returned shortly, casting her a look that conveyed distrust. When he was gone, she reassumed her seat by the door.

Mrs. Thorndike once again offered tea to the doctor, and

he again declined before resuming his story.

"I feel a tremendous responsibility for her death, you see. There was someone across the street she needed to check on, and I'm afraid I was bit short with her. I was quite irritable and distracted, you see, with all that was going on, so I told her to make it quick, then I turned to tend to my patients as she rushed out the door. I hadn't known that outside the hospital entrance there was a crater across which a wooden plank had been placed to allow staff to pass and beneath that plank and within that crater, completely unknown to everyone, lay an unexploded bomb. Missus Piper had already crossed safely, but when she tried to return, it finally exploded at the exact moment she stepped upon the plank. A number of those patients in the basement were buried and killed, and scores more were injured. It took some time for the rescuers to locate her body, what was left of it, that is. But the Germans hadn't quite finished. They returned again later for two more consecutive nights of bombing."

Alice angrily pushed herself away from the wall, where she had been listening, and rushed across the entry hall to a window that faced the front of the building. Throwing herself onto the floor, she sat with her arms crossed and stared out the window, looking but not seeing. She was beyond tears at the moment. She had shed a great many of those in the past few days. She was filled with resentment at the unfairness of it all and angry that now she was delivered against her will to this cold house to live with strangers with whom she would have nothing in common. She hated her life.

Doctor Finlay looked up from the floor where he had been staring.

"Perhaps I will have a bit of tea after all," he said.

"You mustn't blame yourself, Doctor," Mrs. Thorndike comforted him as she poured. "How could you have known that would happen? You didn't even know the bomb was there."

"I suppose you're right, but still ..." he said with a sigh. "So, you see, I feel an obligation to her daughter. The girl's father is off fighting the war somewhere in the Sudan. I haven't been able to locate him, so he doesn't even know his wife has died and his home was destroyed, the poor fellow."

The Doctor took a sip of tea as a cup was handed to him. "The girl should have been evacuated to the countryside along with the other children when the blitz began, but she refused to leave her mother, and her mother couldn't bear to part with her, unfortunately. The little house she lived in was completely destroyed. There are only a couple of relatives, but they live in downtown London. They've had their share of German bombs as well, so there's no point sending her to live with them. Therefore, I am profoundly grateful to Captain Bramwell as well as to you and the rest of the staff for looking after her, at least until my work is finished in Coventry. Hopefully things will settle down a bit there soon and I can return home and to my work here. When I get back, the girl can stay with me until, when and if, her father returns."

"The Captain has instructed us to see to her every need until your return," she assured him. "I'm sorry that we haven't yet been successful in acquiring a teacher for her, and he would prefer not to send her to the little school in the village, so I have acquired a number of books that she can

…"

"I'm sorry," the Doctor interrupted. "What's his objection to the school?"

"It's not the school specifically," she replied, choosing her words carefully. "As you well know, the Captain is passionate about his privacy, and the people of the village are a curious lot. The girl would likely be subject to many uncomfortable questions from the other children about her life here in this house. They believe these grounds are haunted, you see."

"Haunted?"

" … By the Captain."

"Ah," the Doctor said, with an understanding nod as he sipped his tea.

"In any event, since the war has begun, many children not much older than this one have left school to go to work. However, the Captain insists the child be spared manual labor for the time being. He prefers that she concentrate on studies instead."

"As do I," the doctor concurred.

Seated before the front window, Alice's attention was captured by movement outside, near the front of the house. Focusing, she was able to make out the dog, who lay in the path where she had last seen it. It was still staring at the front doorstep, as if expecting her to return.

She had decided to go outside to greet the animal when suddenly a rabbit dashed across its path, and the dog lurched to its feet and gave pursuit, instantly disappearing into the brush. Alice sat back down on the floor, disappointed.

"I haven't seen the Captain for several months," the Doctor continued in the study. "How is he faring?"

"I don't see him, of course," Mrs. Thorndike answered. "He remains down there in his little cottage, all alone except for that dog. Ridley delivers his meals and tends to his needs, but even he rarely actually sees him. Only you are allowed that privilege, of course, on occasion."

The Doctor nodded. Captain Bramwell's life continued unchanged. He knew the Captain's routine. He would close himself in his study and remain there until the butler had finished his chores and departed. Besides her position as housekeeper, a position she occupied with rigid formality, Mrs. Thorndike also maintained his financial records, and the tenants who farmed his land would deal with the Captain through her, but she never saw him either. When she needed to review business matters with him, he always remained concealed behind a partition.

"For 26 years now, he's avoided contact with the outside world," Mrs. Thorndike reflected. "Were it not for you, I doubt he could have made it. You've kept him alive, you know."

"No," the Doctor said with a shake of his head. "It was the dog, Missus Thorndike. The dog has kept him alive."

He hastily took a final sip before he returned his cup to the tray and stood.

"I'd like to see him before I go, so if you'll excuse me …"

"Of course," she said as she stood and rang for Ridley before escorting her guest to the door.

The Doctor paused before leaving the room.

"Missus Thorndike," he said to her, "I expect the girl to receive the best of attention under your care. I don't expect her to be terribly difficult, but she can sometimes be a bit headstrong and independent, though I must confess I rather admire that about her."

He paused to smile as he reflected on her personality. "However, you'll also find her to be very intelligent and delightful company. I've grown quite fond of her, and I trust you will treat her with fairness and sensitivity. Remember that she has just lost her mother, and right now she's likely to feel terribly alone and confused."

Mrs. Thorndike bristled.

"Doctor Finlay, I am *always* fair."

"Of course, you are," the Doctor replied, suppressing a smile.

The two of them proceeded into the entry hall, where they found Alice, still seated on the floor before the window. She did not acknowledge their presence. The Doctor accepted his hat and coat from Ridley as he observed her with a look of concern.

"Alice, Doctor Finlay is leaving now," Mrs. Thorndike called out to her. "Please say your goodbye."

"I would think that you and your staff should address her with the same formality you would extend to any other guest," the Doctor said to the housekeeper. "'Miss Piper' will do."

Mrs. Thorndike smiled slightly. "She's only a child, Doctor. We mustn't forget that."

Before he could respond, Alice suddenly stood and rushed to him, embracing him tightly.

"Please don't leave me here," she said to him quietly.

"You'll be fine," he assured her as he patted her back. "I promise, and I'll be back to fetch you in no time at all."

She continued to hold him.

"Come, my dear," Mrs. Thorndike finally said to her. "We mustn't keep Doctor Finlay from his work."

When Alice still held firm, the Doctor awkwardly removed her arms from around his waist, and she reluctantly complied.

"There's a good girl, now," he said to her.

With a final goodbye to Mrs. Thorndike, he was gone.

CHAPTER THREE

"Now then. My name is Missus Thorndike, and I will look after you during your stay with us," the housekeeper introduced herself as soon as the Doctor had left. Turning to Ridley, she ordered him to summon the staff.

She tapped the side of Alice's suitcase with the toe of her shoe and asked, "Is this all you brought with you?"

Alice nodded. She had already formed a dislike for this lady, her stiff formality and coldness. It was obvious to her that Mrs. Thorndike would have no fondness for her either.

"I don't suppose you've had your supper?" Mrs. Thorndike asked but didn't wait for a response. "You shall dine in the kitchen with the staff and me."

"There's a dog outside," Alice interrupted quietly.

"What?" Missus Thorndike asked. She had heard the girl but couldn't comprehend what her question had to do with anything.

"When I arrived," the girl said, "I saw a dog outside. Is it yours?"

"Heavens, *no!*" Mrs. Thorndike exclaimed, an expression of absolute horror on her face. "I never go near that beast. Now pay attention to me and don't let your mind wander. We have rules here that I expect you to obey, so listen carefully to what I have to say so you don't get into any trouble."

"Will I need paper and pencil?" Alice asked.

"Will you need ... ?" the housekeeper stammered, her face screwed into a look of disbelief.

"I want to know if I should write down what you say, so I won't get into any trouble."

Alice liked to tease those who took themselves too seriously. Often when she encountered such personalities, she would play with them by seeming to be naïve and foolish. It amused her to see the frustration that resulted.

Mrs. Thorndike's expression turned to a frown. She recognized the girl's game and would have nothing of it. She ignored the question.

Ridley returned, accompanied by a robust lady in her 50's dressed in a cook's apron, who was introduced as Mrs. Belmore, and a slightly younger, thin, sour-faced maid named Anna. Alice didn't think any of them looked happy.

"We'll put the girl in the Grey Room on the third floor," Mrs. Thorndike told the staff. "It's not very large so it will be easier to clean, and there's a desk where she can study and a window that will allow for fresh air, which should please Doctor Finlay. From the look of her, she could use a bit of it. Probably spent her life inhaling those toxic fumes from the factories, no doubt."

The staff looked at their new guest with disapproval.

"I won't be any trouble," Alice said to them. "I promise." Her declaration failed to win them over.

"Set a place for her at the kitchen table," Mrs. Thorndike instructed the cook. "I'll show her to her room and see that she's settled. That will be all."

The staff departed and without looking at her, Mrs. Thorndike instructed Alice to follow her. The girl picked up her suitcase and proceeded up the stairway.

"So far," Alice thought, "I haven't seen this lady smile even once." She wondered if she could change that but dismissed the thought. She was not Pollyanna.

As they proceeded past the second floor, she noticed the halls of closed doors.

"Does anyone stay in these rooms?" she asked.

Mrs. Thorndike took her time before replying. "No," she answered.

"There seem to be so many," Alice mused.

"You'll be seeing no one but the staff and me while you are with us," Mrs. Thorndike told her. "You must avoid socializing with the groundskeeper should you encounter him outside as well as any visitors who may drop in to conduct business." She paused to address Alice directly. "If, at any time you should encounter Captain Bramwell, you are to look away and under no circumstances are you to speak to him, do I make myself clear?"

"But what if he should speak to me first?" Alice asked. "It would be impolite to ignore him."

"That won't happen, I assure you."

"Why mustn't I even look at him? He'll think me discourteous."

"Trust me, girl. You will not wish to look at him."

Mrs. Thorndike continued up the stairs and said with finality, "That's all we'll say on the subject. Ever."

Alice shrugged and followed. It had been her second warning about Captain Bramwell. Now she was challenged.

Mrs. Thorndike paused on the third floor before a door at the top of the stairway and thumbed through a collection of keys on a ring she withdrew from her pocket. The hinges creaked noticeably as she unlocked the door and entered.

Alice stood in the doorway surveying the room as Mrs.

Thorndike proceeded to remove sheets from the furniture, which consisted of a wardrobe, a chest of drawers, a nightstand and a chair and desk, which faced the wall near a window. A white bedcover was spread across the medium-sized four-poster bed, which, along with the white window curtains, stood out sharply against the dismal, gray-colored walls. To Alice, the room seemed large compared to the tiny bedroom she had occupied in the small flat in which she had been raised.

Mrs. Thorndike unlatched and opened the casements, admitting a light, cool breeze, which Alice found too brisk for her sensibilities. She'd wait for Mrs. Thorndike to leave before she closed them.

"A set of schoolbooks will be delivered tomorrow," Alice was told. "You can use them for your studies while you are with us, and I will review your work."

Alice looked out the window and was pleased to find that it offered an ample view of the grounds in front of the house.

"You may remove your coat and scarf and hang them up in the wardrobe," Mrs. Thorndike instructed her as she lifted her suitcase onto the bed and unstrapped the gas mask that had been attached.

"You won't be needing this *here*," she said disdainfully as she tossed it aside before examining the contents of the suitcase.

"Trousers?" Mrs. Thorndike asked as she held two pair up for inspection.

"Yes, they are," Alice replied as she put her coat away.

"Only two pair of boys' trousers?" Mrs. Thorndike

asked. "Didn't you bring any girls' clothing with you?"

"I have this one," Alice said as she referred to the worn, one-piece dress she was wearing. "It was all I could salvage. Our home was destroyed, remember? The fire brigade wouldn't let me back in after it was damaged. I had to sneak in when no one was looking, and I grabbed all I could find before I was caught and made to leave."

Mrs. Thorndike came across a copy of the book *Doctor Dolittle's Return,* and after glancing at the cover, she tossed it next to the gas mask and continued rummaging through the suitcase, removing a toothbrush, comb, socks, slippers and a pair of underclothing that she laid out upon the bed. After sorting through the small remainder of other items, expressing a "tsk tsk," and a couple of gasps and sighs of disgust, she pushed the suitcase away from her.

"Very well, then," she said. "Put away these wretched things for now. Day after tomorrow we shall have to go into the village and purchase a new wardrobe. This will simply never do."

Alice hugged her arms as she felt the chill of the early evening breeze blowing through the window.

"But I don't mind. I'm very comfortable wearing trousers," she said.

"You can hardly wear trousers to church," Mrs. Thorndike told her. "During your stay here, you'll dress as a young lady should. That's an end to the matter."

Mrs. Thorndike looked disdainfully at Alice's hair, which was pulled behind her ears into tangled curls that reached the base of her neck. Only the bangs on her forehead appeared to have been combed.

"We must do something about *that* as well," she said, and then she glanced at a small watch she pulled from her pocket. "It's nearly time for supper. Anna will summon you when it's ready. You'll find the bathroom located at the end of the hall."

She turned to leave, and Alice looked out the window once more.

"I always wanted a dog," Alice said. "Father promised to get me one just as soon as he comes home."

Mrs. Thorndike stood at the door, visually evaluating her for a moment, then shook her head and left.

Alice closed the casements and ran to sit on the bed, bouncing on it to test its softness. She judged it to be sufficient but as she sat looking about the quiet, dreary room, she suddenly felt very much alone. A wave of depression swept over her.

Barely an hour later, there was a soft knock on her door, and Anna called her to supper. The maid said nothing to Alice as she followed her downstairs and into the lower quarters of the house to a small kitchen, where five settings had been placed. Alice was seated next to Anna, and when the food was served, Mrs. Thorndike entered the kitchen, and all the staff was seated. After Mrs. Thorndike delivered a simple prayer of thanks, the meal was consumed silently.

Alice normally would have been disposed to initiate a conversation and make an attempt to lighten the mood, but the melancholy that had overtaken her earlier had not passed. Though the food she was offered was agreeable enough, her mood inhibited her appetite, and she could not bring herself to eat.

"Why aren't you eating, girl?" Mrs. Thorndike asked as she noticed Alice toying with her food. "Is the food not to your liking?"

"No, ma'am," Alice replied. "I'm not hungry, that's all."

"You'll be hungry enough by morning, I'll wager," Mrs. Thorndike warned her.

Alice tried, very slowly, to eat some of the food, but her effort was of little use. By the time the others had finished, Alice's meal remained only half eaten.

"Very well," Mrs. Thorndike said to her, "if you will not eat then you had best retire to your room. I shall be up later to check on you and turn out your light. You are dismissed."

Back in her room, Alice rushed to the window to see if the dog had returned, but there was just enough light before the gathering dusk to reveal to her that it had not. Disappointed, she threw herself onto her bed and lay for some time, wishing she could fall asleep, anything to make the world go away, but her wish was in vain. Finally giving up, she turned on the light on the small nightstand and picked up the book that was still lying on the bed, hoping she could lose herself in the exploits of Doctor Dolittle. She had read the book twice already, but it was all she had at hand and would have to do.

Mrs. Thorndike dropped in to announce bedtime earlier than Alice expected, and after brushing her teeth and preparing for bed, she settled in beneath the bedcovers that had been turned down for her.

After turning out the nightstand lamp and moving the book to the desk, Mrs. Thorndike paused at the door to scan the room. Satisfied that all was in order, she said a perfunctory "Good night" and switched off the light. As she left, she purposefully left the door ajar a few inches, which allowed a very slim, faint, stream of light from somewhere down the hall to fall upon the floor. After a few minutes the source of that light was extinguished, leaving a beam of moonlight as the only source of illumination in the room as it radiated through the window and cast its glow across the bed.

In the silence and darkness of the room, Alice's loneliness intensified. Though she had long fought against it, she couldn't stop herself from crying. She gave herself permission to cry only when no one else could see her and now, with visions of her mother and father overwhelming her, she clutched her pillow and yielded to her emotions. Knowing she would never see her mother again, she called out to her, questioning why she had to leave and wishing against all logic for her to come back. Alice's only hope was that her father would return from the war and rescue her from the bleak conditions to which she had been delivered. It was nearly an hour later before she finally and forlornly fell asleep amid the many tears that dampened her pillow.

Much later that evening, long after the remaining lights in the house had been extinguished and the rest of the household had retired, as the time very nearly approached 11 PM, Alice awoke.

It may have been the unfamiliarity of her new surroundings that made her uneasy and prevented her from sleeping soundly, or she may have been haunted by her imagination, triggered by the eerie words of warning she had been given earlier that day about the mysterious Captain Bramwell. More likely it was a sound she could hear coming from outside her room as something ascended the stairway and crept its way across the carpeted floor leading to her door. She couldn't identify the sound, but she knew it wasn't human, and she drew her blanket up above her head. It was a trick she had acquired on nights when her mother had to work late at the hospital, and she was left alone to care for herself. She would curl her body up into a ball, bury her face in the pillow and cover her head with her blanket so that if some mysterious monster crept into her room she would present as small a silhouette as possible, hoping that Frankenstein or Dracula would not see her in the darkness and would pass her by. Alice and her school friends were all far too young to be allowed to see scary movies, but there was always one boy in the group who delighted in describing to the others the appearance and behaviour of the movie monsters he himself hadn't even seen, making them even more frightening than they were depicted at the cinema. At that moment, Alice was certain that one of them, exactly as she imagined one to be, was about to enter her room, and she shivered.

She could discern a heavy panting sound outside her room, and soon she could hear the squeaking of the hinges as the door was slowly pushed open a few inches wider. Alice would have screamed, but the specter she envisioned of Mrs. Thorndike responding to her plea for help and entering her room in the darkness would be no less frightening than the situation she was presently facing. She tried to breathe quietly by taking shallow breaths, so the phantom would not hear her in the darkness, but she couldn't muffle the sound of her heartbeat, which she was sure could be heard for some distance.

Alice feared that the thing that stood in her doorway was

the mysterious Captain Bramwell himself, come to frighten the new visitor whom he had not yet seen. Should she order him to leave her room, she wondered? What would he do to her if she dared look upon him? Could she possibly be dreaming?

The intruder could be heard crossing the floor, coming nearer as it approached her bedside and then stopping there for a moment, as if expecting Alice to acknowledge its presence. When no response was given, there was a sudden pressure placed on the bed near her feet and the bedsprings squeaked under the weight. Was the thing leaning upon her bed, she puzzled? If so, it wasn't quite as large as she envisioned it must be.

Whatever the creature might have been, it dropped an object on the bed near her waist, and then waited, as if expecting a response from Alice, but for nearly one minute she gave none.

Finally, she could stand the tension no longer. Holding her breath, she threw her blankets back and sat upright, eyes wide with fear. But the sight she beheld was not at all what she expected, and she exhaled a forceful breath of relief.

There at her bedside, his tail wagging as he waited recognition, sat the collie she had seen earlier and had so wished to see again. As he panted, his open mouth seemed to form a smile as his kind, almond-shaped brown eyes looked hopefully into hers. One white foot rested beside her on the bed, and near his paw lay a red cricket ball that he had dropped there as an invitation to play.

As soon as Alice collected herself, she began laughing excitedly as she simultaneously attempted to catch her breath.

It was the first time she had laughed since her mother had died.

"You silly, silly boy!" she said to the dog. "You are a boy, aren't you? I can't imagine a girl dog causing such a fright! My heart very nearly stopped beating, you silly, silly …"

The dog barked back at her, and she quickly shushed him.

"Shh!" she said, lowering her voice. "You mustn't wake Missus Thorndike! She hates dogs. She told me so, and, well, who knows what she might do if she finds you here!"

She wasn't certain where Mrs. Thorndike and the others slept, but she hoped it was far enough from her room that even the dog's bark couldn't be heard.

Alice took his face in her hands, and as she scratched his ears she began laughing again, and like the warm, comforting touch of the dog's silky fur, it felt very good. After a few enjoyable moments, he pulled his muzzle away and used it to nudge the ball toward her.

"Oh, of course!" Alice exclaimed. "You want to play with the ball! That's why you came to see me, isn't it? How on earth did you get into the house? Well, no matter."

Tossing aside her covers, she picked up the cricket ball and teased him with it a moment before tossing it low to the floor toward the wall. The ball bounced lightly two times before hitting the wall and bouncing back. The dog swiftly jumped toward it and caught it mid-air.

"It's not a very good ball for a dog to play fetch, is it?" Alice asked as the dog lifted his front paws on the side of the bed and dropped the ball before her again. "Still, you fetch very well, don't you? I know! Missus Thorndike will be taking me to the village to buy some new clothes. Perhaps I can find you a new ball, something with some bounce in it. You'd like that, wouldn't you?"

The collie licked her cheek in response.

"You should be given a reward for being such a good dog," she said with a laugh. "Perhaps I can sneak a biscuit from my supper tomorrow, but I must be very careful, or Missus Thorndike might catch me. You'd like a good biscuit, wouldn't you?

The dog barked, and she laughed as she shushed him again and tossed the ball once more.

She began a competition with him, racing to see who could retrieve the ball first, and the two of them delightedly continued their game for several minutes more until Alice, fatigued, jumped onto the bed and leaned back against her pillow.

"Perhaps we should rest for a while," she said to the dog.

As if understanding, he jumped onto the bed and crawled up next to her, still holding the ball in his mouth, repeatedly allowing it to drop on the bed and promptly scooping it up again. Alice lay next to him, her arm around his velvety white neck as she cuddled close. The dog finally dropped the ball and licked her cheek before resting his head between his paws, breathing a long, exhausted moan, which caused Alice to chuckle.

"You'll stay with me, won't you?" she asked very softly into his ear. "I need you to stay with me."

The girl's breath tickled his ear as she whispered, and he

shook his head and brushed it with his paw. His reaction caused her to giggle once again before she slowly drifted into sleep, feeling secure and calm. A smile never left her face. The collie soon followed her into sleep.

The two of them remained so occupied until the large grandfather clock in the entry hall downstairs struck midnight. Alice didn't hear the chimes ring, but she and the collie were suddenly wakened by another sound. It was an odd, distant whistle, coming from somewhere outside the house, and it seemed to be calling someone.

The dog raised his head and lay still for a moment until the whistle was repeated, and then jumped from the bed and headed for the door.

"Wait!" Alice called to him, but he didn't respond. "You forgot your ball!" she called frantically as she held it in her hand. The dog was nearly out the door before he stopped and turned to her. She tossed the ball, which he again caught in mid-air before rushing out the door.

As Alice heard the dog's footsteps retreating down the stairs, she heard the whistle outside repeated, and she rushed to the window. Through the glass she observed the courtyard, illuminated by the radiance of the full, setting moon, and she could see the silhouettes of the trees and outbuildings at its edge. As she gazed at the scene, she perceived the shadow of a lone figure, standing at the head of the dirt path where she had first seen the collie.

The man, as Alice determined he must be, was tall, but he stood slightly stooped. He wore a heavy dark overcoat, and his head was concealed by a large, broad-brimmed hat that cast a shadow over his face and rendered his features impossible to ascertain. His right arm hung loosely at his side while the other held onto an underarm crutch.

Alice was certain it must be Captain Bramwell, and a chill ran through her as she imagined what his face might look like in the light of day.

As she watched, she saw the collie, wagging his tail, rush merrily across the distance from the house to greet him, and as they met, the man, seemingly ignoring the dog, turned to walk up the path as the dog led the way. Despite the aid of the crutch, the man walked with much difficulty, and the dog slowed his pace in order to remain close to him.

After a few awkward steps, the man suddenly stopped, slowly turned, and gazed up at the house. Alice was certain he was looking at her window. After a moment, he turned back and gradually faded into the darkness.

CHAPTER FOUR

Alice was already awake when Anna knocked on her door the next morning. Her sleep the previous night was more a series of naps clouded with nightmares of shadowy figures, ghosts and monsters. She was startled awake from each fearful dream by a vision of the grim figure of the man she had seen at midnight, who would slowly lift his lifeless right arm, allowing his coat sleeve to pull back, revealing the limb beneath to be nothing more than a skeleton. As he pointed a long, skeletal finger directly at her, she would awaken in a sweat, only to have the vision repeat itself each time she managed to fall back asleep.

Only one thing gave her comfort and made even brief periods of rest possible: It was the memory of the collie and the moment of happiness he had brought her. She was soothed by the rationalization that such a kind and sweet animal would not willingly live with someone who was thoroughly evil. Captain Bramwell, as she assumed the man to be, could not really be the dreadful ogre she imagined, and she was reminded of the story of *Beauty and the Beast* that her mother used to tell her. Deep within the chest of the Captain must beat the heart of a kind and gentle man, she reasoned. Each time she arrived at that perception, however, a contradictory dream would creep over her, as if she were being given a grim warning.

After knocking twice, Anna opened the door.

"Missus Thorndike wishes to see you in the study downstairs," she said, not looking directly at Alice. "She asks that you please be quick." After a pause, she added, "*Before* breakfast," then left.

Alice considered the order. Did it sound as if she were in some sort of trouble? How could that be, she wondered? She hadn't left her room all night. Perhaps Missus Thorndike knew about the dog. Alice determined to face whatever consequences lay ahead with resolve. What else could happen to her, she thought? Might she be sent back to Coventry? Would the bombing be more frightening than the wrath of Mrs. Thorndike and the bogeyman who owned the estate?

Taking inventory of her wardrobe, she opted for the trousers. "If I'm in trouble," she thought, "I might as well be comfortable."

Shortly thereafter she was knocking at Mrs. Thorndike's door and was admitted into the study, where she found the head housekeeper writing in a log. She did not acknowledge Alice.

"You wished to see me?" Alice finally asked.

Mrs. Thorndike finished her entry before laying aside her pen and closing the logbook. Noticing Alice's choice in clothing brought a frown of displeasure to her face.

"I trust you slept well?" she asked.

Alice gave a slight shrug.

"Last night you had little interest in your supper," Mrs. Thorndike continued. "How does your appetite fare this morning?"

"Well enough," Alice replied with a nod.

Mrs. Thorndike reacted with mock disbelief. "I should have thought you satisfied your appetite during the night."

Alice looked at her with a puzzled look on her face.

"In the kitchen?" Mrs. Thorndike said, prompting her.

"After everyone else had retired for the evening?"

"I have no idea what you're talking about," Alice replied, bewildered.

"Don't play games with me, girl," Mrs. Thorndike said, her anger growing. "You left your room last night, found your way downstairs to the kitchen and made off with several items that, I suspect, you consumed in your room."

"I did no such thing!" Alice exclaimed fiercely.

"You will not raise your voice with me," Mrs. Thorndike warned her. "Missus Belmore keeps very accurate records of her inventory. She has been employed in this house for nearly 30 years and during all that time there has never once been a theft in her kitchen. Not until last night, your first night here. Need I remind you we are at war? All of our food is very tightly rationed, and we cannot abide waste of any kind."

"I never left my room last night! How dare you call me a thief!"

Mrs. Thorndike stood, glaring at Alice. "You will have no need for breakfast this morning," she said after collecting herself. "You will return to your room, where you will remain until mid-day. Anna will summon you for lunch at that time. You may leave now."

As Alice stood staring at her, there was a knock on the door and Ridley entered.

"If I may have a word?" he asked Mrs. Thorndike.

"You have been dismissed, girl!" she said to Alice, sharply.

Alice turned on her heel but stopped at the door and turned back her.

"Oh. You needn't remind me we are at war," Alice said to her heatedly, fighting back tears of anger. "This war killed my mother, you may recall! And *you* may address me by my proper name. My name is Alice. Not 'girl.' Not 'child.' If you wish my respect, I am entitled to respect from you. I'm sure Doctor Finlay would agree!"

She left the room, slamming the door behind her.

Mrs. Thorndike placed a hand on her desk, as if to catch her balance, and used her other hand to cover her mouth, which was open wide with shock.

Ridley stood uneasily for a moment, waiting for permission to speak.

"Missus Thorndike?" he finally asked. "Are you all right?"

"What is it, Ridley?" she finally managed to respond.

"Well, ma'am, Missus Belmore has completed her inventory of the kitchen provisions," he informed her. "It appears that in addition to the items she reported to you this morning, there are several other items missing."

Mrs. Thorndike threw herself into her chair with exasperation.

"That wretched child!" she proclaimed. "She shall be the death of me. I can see that already."

"But that's what Missus Belmore wished me to report," Ridley said. "Among the missing items were some portions of meat and canned goods."

"What has that ...?" she started to ask.

"You see, it's unlikely the young lady would have the proper tool to open the canned goods, nor the means with which to cook the meat," Ridley pointed out.

Mrs. Thorndike thought over his comment carefully.

"We also noticed the outside entrance to the kitchen was unlocked this morning. Of course, there is always the possibility that it was left unlocked by one of the staff," he added.

"Unlikely," Mrs. Thorndike replied. "Missus Belmore is responsible for locking the kitchen door before retiring. I rely on her."

"Perhaps someone from the village was able to pick the lock. Shall I telephone the Constable?"

"No! No!" she responded emphatically, raising a hand. "The Captain would be furious with us. News of the Constable's visit would surely reach the villagers. Who knows what they might make of it. No, we'd best keep this matter private until we can learn more ourselves. Meanwhile, we'll watch the girl closely. I'm still not entirely convinced she isn't responsible in some way."

Returning to her room, Alice threw herself onto her bed and began angrily striking it with her fists. Any thought of crying was obscured by the anger and frustration she was feeling. She vowed to herself that she would cry no more. She believed it was getting in the way of rational thinking, and at least until her father returned from the war, she must keep all her wits about her and keep herself strong if she were to stand up to Mrs. Thorndike, and even to the Captain, if it came to it. She had no one to rely on for support but herself.

Of one thing she was certain. She would not remain confined to her room all morning. Jumping from the bed she stomped to the window and surveyed the grounds outside.

The allure of such a beautiful spring day could not be ignored. Alice was confident she could sneak out of the house and manage to return before noon undetected, and she hastened to obtain her coat and blue scarf from the wardrobe. She resolved to find the one friend she had in this wretched place. She would find the collie.

Quietly, and ever so cautiously, she descended the stairs, stopping only once when she encountered Anna, holding a rag and feather duster as she passed through the second-floor hallway. Alice, leaning closely to the wall, waited unnoticed, concealed behind a Greek statue of a woman. When Anna had passed, Alice resumed her escape.

At the bottom of the stairs, she found the door to the study was closed. Considering an escape out the front door too risky, she chose instead to make her way down a hallway beside the staircase that appeared to lead to the back of the house. Traveling carefully along the passage she found several doors closed while some were not, including one that opened into a grand dining room.

Continuing further down the hall, she noticed what appeared to be an outside light emanating from beneath a sizeable set of double doors. She carefully opened one, and discovered what appeared to be a spacious ballroom. The opposite wall of the room consisted entirely of many large panes of glass from floor to ceiling through which the morning sun radiated, brilliantly illuminating the room. The windows were framed with magnificent white curtains, but what caught her eye was the set of French doors located directly center.

Silently closing the door behind her, Alice rushed across

the floor and opened the glass doors that opened onto a small patio, which, in turn, led into a modest garden. She paused briefly to pull a portion of a curtain across the door opening to prevent it from closing completely, enabling her access from the outside on her return. Then she rushed out enthusiastically.

Making her way through the garden area, she came to a hedge that completely encircled the area, designating its boundary. Pausing, she looked beyond the periphery, past a green field to the edge of a thick growth of trees. There she spotted her objective: the dirt path that led past the house and stables and wound its way beyond, to what would surely be the Captain's cottage. It was there, or in that area, that she hoped to find the collie. Leaping over the hedge, she approached the path.

Traveling the lane, she found it soon led through a narrow gap in the trees and then continued deep into their midst. Screwing up her courage, she advanced.

After a brief walk, she found the pathway led past the edge of a small lake that was populated by various waterfowl and that contained an area of thick reeds and lilies that grew unattended near its center. The water was dark, but its surface shimmered with the glare of the morning sun, and a small, aged gazebo sat at its edge near the pathway. A little rusted metal garden table and two chairs sat in the center, and ivy grew thickly neglected about the structure. Its abandoned appearance and the lack of a lane approaching it indicated it had not been in use for many years. A shoddy, run-down rowboat rested on the shore. The general atmosphere left Alice with a feeling that the location was haunted, and because she also harbored a fear of water, she was grateful

41

when the path eventually steered away from the lake and back into the trees.

It was only after traveling a few hundred meters that Alice arrived at a clearing, and within its center sat a small, bleak and weathered cottage. There was a slim gravel pathway leading to a single door and a few curtained windows against which blinds were half drawn, and the cottage backed up to the edge of a dark, imposing forest into which no access was visible. All was quiet save for a lonely wind that blew through the treetops and the sound of a few birds chirping somewhere in the distance. How could the sweet collie she met ever know true happiness living in such a dreary dwelling, she wondered. She remained at the edge for a moment, taking in the scene before her and deciding on her next move.

Alice knew calling or whistling for the dog might catch the attention of the resident, so instead she decided to venture on, hoping to at least make visual contact. Though her primary goal was to see the collie again, she was also possessed of a compelling curiosity to get a closer view of the Captain and to learn for herself what it was about him that others kept warning her against.

Slowly and stealthily drawing nearer the cottage, she could see no movement or sign of life. Perhaps the resident was in a back room, she thought, or perhaps he was still asleep after having been up so late the previous evening scaring little girls. She was determined not to allow herself to be frightened *this* time.

Ducking low, she knelt beneath one of the two front windows and then gradually lifted her head to peer inside.

The room within was dimly lit, and its features were visible only due to what little light shined its way through the half-closed blinds.

Alice could see that the room was sparsely furnished save for a desk and chair, and, in one corner, a large, thickly upholstered leather chair beside which a table and reading lamp resided. A pipe sat upon the table as if it had just recently been placed there, and next to it was a pair of wire-rimmed reading glasses to which an elastic band had been attached, reaching from the back of one temple earpiece to the other, apparently to make it possible for them to fit securely around the head of someone who had neither ears nor nose, or so Alice imagined.

Bookcases occupied every wall and were completely crammed with books, top to bottom. Alice had never seen so many books at one time in one place, and she wondered how many years it would take for someone to read them all.

Her investigation came to a sudden stop when she heard a man's cough nearby from somewhere outside, and she sat frozen and scarcely breathing as she tried to identify the source of the sound. It must have come from somewhere behind the cottage, she decided, and crouching low, she carefully crept in that direction, clinging close to the wall. Reaching the corner of the building, she cautiously peeked around its edge.

Eventually she was able to clearly see a man on a wooden porch with his back to her staring into the darkness of the ominous forest whose boundary began several meters away from the back of the cottage. The crutch he was leaning on with his left arm confirmed to her that he was Captain

Bramwell. He was casually dressed, and she noticed that his right leg, against which his right arm hung so lifelessly, was slightly shorter than the left. He also wore a black cotton scarf wrapped around his head. Next to his side, lay the collie, panting as he also watched the edge of the forest.

Alice did her best to remain quiet and still so as not to draw the attention of the pair, but her effort was in vain. The dog suddenly stopped panting and turned his head in her direction. She quickly pulled her head from view, but she was too late. With a loud bark, the collie leapt to his feet and ran toward her. She turned to run away, but as she did so, she couldn't resist one glance at the man on the porch. She immediately regretted the impulse as Captain Bramwell whipped his head around to see what attracted the dog's attention. He instantaneously grabbed the right edge of the scarf that encircled his head and drew it across his face, leaving only his left eye visible.

In the split second it took for him to conceal himself, Alice was unable to fully comprehend what she had seen, so unbelievable were his features, and in that brief moment her mind denied what her eyes had seen. She was left with only a vague, inhuman image that defied categorization. She stood for a moment, paralyzed with shock.

"What in hell are you doing here, you disobedient little idiot?" He yelled at her in a loud, gravelly voice. "Damn you! Keep away! Keep away from me before I break your foolish little neck!"

It was enough to snap her out of her paralysis and send her scrambling away, screaming in fear. She was aware that the dog was running with her, barking with excitement, as

Captain Bramwell hurled curses at her from the porch. She had never heard many of the words he used, and as she raced away from the cottage she heard him call for the collie.

"Banner! Banner, come back here!" he commanded, and the dog stopped.

Alice stored the name somewhere in the back of her mind to digest later, but at that moment her one thought was to get back to the house and into her room. Was there a lock on her bedroom door, she tried to remember?

She had never run so fast in her life, and it took very little time for her to make her way back into the house, throwing all caution aside as she bounded up the stairs, two steps at a time, startling Anna along the way, who barely had time to step out of her path to keep from being knocked down.

Inside her room, she concealed herself in the wardrobe, closing the door tightly. After a few minutes, however, she couldn't stand the darkness and the lack of air, and she opened the door just a crack before lowering herself to cower on the floor, breathing heavily and trying to calm her shaking body.

"Banner!" she thought to herself. "I need Banner to keep me safe!"

CHAPTER FIVE

Alice hoped that Banner would return to her room that night, but when he didn't, she wasn't surprised.

Lunch had been a silent affair, and she was grateful that Anna had apparently not told Mrs. Thorndike about their encounter on the stairs that morning. The rest of the day was spent in her room perusing the textbooks that had been delivered, but her mind was not on her studies. Supper was similarly somber, though Alice made some effort at conversation.

"Doesn't anyone …," she began, drawing scowls of disapproval from the staff.

"Doesn't anyone ever go anywhere or do anything?" she continued.

"What would you have us do?" Mrs. Thorndike asked.

"Oh, I don't know," Alice replied. "Social gatherings, dances, parties and such? Don't you have friends or relatives you visit? Do you spend all of your time in this house?"

"This is not the time for social activities," Mrs. Thorndike stated icily. "Our country is at war."

With that statement, the meal continued in silence.

Sleep did not come easily to Alice again that night. She worried that the wicked Captain Bramwell might be lurking in the darkness of the house somewhere, waiting for the opportunity to sneak into her room to terrorize her. She couldn't get him off her mind and she wondered if he could really be the monster he appeared to be. Did Banner see something in his soul that wasn't obvious to anyone else, something that made life with him tolerable? She had been told that dogs were supposed to be good judges of character, and she preferred to believe that, but still she wondered.

The night did not pass without one visitor, and it was not Banner. Late that night she was awakened by a movement near her bed, and when she opened her eyes she immediately noticed that the door to her room was opened wider than it had been when she had been put to sleep.

For a moment she lay still, trying to identify the sound. At first she thought it might be Banner, but the more she listened, the more she was certain it was human. She could tell that someone was kneeling beside her bed, searching for something beneath it, and she could hear what she thought must be a hand, sweeping the wooden floor as it explored the surface.

With a sudden movement, she jerked herself into a sitting position, and as she did so, the intruder raised her head and Alice screamed with alarm as she beheld Mrs. Thorndike's stern face just inches from her own. If she had been wakened by a witch, Alice couldn't have been more startled.

"Hush, you silly child!" Mrs. Thorndike hissed at her. "You'll wake the entire household!"

"What are you doing?" Alice gasped.

"You know very well what I'm doing," she grumbled as she pulled herself to her feet and walked to the door.

Pausing there, she looked back at Alice and said, "I don't care what the staff believes, *I'm* certain you've hidden the food you stole somewhere in this room, and when I find it, you can be sure Captain Bramwell will send you away, perhaps to an institution for orphaned children who steal!"

With a triumphant look, she turned on her heel and left the room, being careful to leave the door slightly ajar.

Alice wasn't certain that an orphanage for children who steal actually existed, but if it did, she thought Mrs. Thorndike would probably run it.

At breakfast the next morning, Mrs. Thorndike abruptly slapped a piece of paper and a pencil next to Alice's plate.

"Write down what size clothes you wear," she ordered as she glanced at the trousers Alice was wearing. "I'm going into the village this morning to purchase something proper for you to wear to church tomorrow."

"Aren't I going with you today?" Alice asked.

"I think it best that you remain here," she was told. "The village is very small. You'll attract attention. I shouldn't want you to be embarrassed."

"Oh, I wouldn't be embarrassed at all, Missus Thorndike. In fact, I love to …"

"Write down the information I asked for and eat your breakfast," Mrs. Thorndike said with finality. "You can spend the morning with your studies and then in the afternoon you will be free to do as you like, so long as you don't get into any trouble, of course."

Afraid to look her in the eye, Alice stammered as she started to make a request of her, but thought better of it and paused, then began again. "I wonder …?"

"What? Out with it, girl!" Mrs. Thorndike demanded impatiently.

"Well," Alice started again, meekly, "I have some small change saved up. I wonder if you could bring back a ball, a rubber ball, perhaps even a tennis ball or something of the sort, something with some bounce in it. You know what I mean?"

"No, I haven't the foggiest," Mrs. Thorndike replied. "And your ignorance astounds me! Rubber has been rationed along with everything else. Rubber ball indeed! Now ..." She nodded and pointed to the pencil and paper.

"I only know my shoe size, I'm afraid," Alice said, lifting the pencil. "I'm not certain about my other sizes. My mother always purchased my clothes."

"Well, I hope your mother had better taste when she shopped for her own."

Mrs. Belmore looked up suddenly from her breakfast with an expression of shock. She glanced at Alice to see how that remark had been received before resuming her meal.

Alice was doing her best to contain her anger.

"We didn't have a lot of money, Missus Thorndike," she said, barely concealing her temper, "especially after my father went off to war, but my mother did the very best she could under the circumstances. Can you say the same of your own mother?"

"How dare you, you impertinent little brat!" Mrs. Thorndike reacted with indignation. For a moment she stared at Alice with eyes wide, nearly trembling with outrage, but noticing that the adults at the table were watching her, she managed to rein in her emotion.

"Write down whatever sizes you are sure of," she said with a shaky voice. "I'll guess at the rest. Rationing has become so strict, there likely won't be much to choose from anyway. Whatever I can obtain will surely be better than anything in your current wardrobe."

Rather than focus on her studies, Alice spent most of the morning pacing her room, pausing occasionally to gaze out her window. The nightmare vision of the Captain's face continued to haunt her, but each time she tried to remember his image clearly, it only became more clouded until she was not at all sure what she had seen. She had so many questions about him and no one to ask.

Mrs. Thorndike was not present for the mid-day meal and though there was still no conversation, the staff seemed slightly more relaxed. Bored, but relaxed. When they had finished, Anna and Ridley retired to their respective rooms, leaving the cleaning of the dishes for later, and Mrs. Belmore went outside through the kitchen door. Left alone, Alice helped herself to an additional biscuit from a dish on the table, concealing it in her pants pocket. She hoped it would remain fresh until she encountered Banner again.

Outside the kitchen door, she passed Mrs. Belmore, who was sitting on a large, upended crate, enjoying a cigarette and a cup of tea. Alice wasn't sure if she was supposed to notice her. She had never seen her smoking when Mrs. Thorndike was around, and, indeed, had never even seen her take a break from her work, so she merely cast her a smile in passing.

"We know it weren't you what's been stealin' the goods," Mrs. Belmore said after Alice passed by.

"I beg your pardon?" Alice said as she stopped and faced her.

"Naw, the old lady's got a bug up her arse," Mrs. Belmore scoffed as she took a puff on her cigarette.

"Somethin' else I been meanin' to tell ya. My boy, my Donald. 'E's off fightin' the Jerries like your own dad. Could be the two of 'em are mates. Who knows? 'E's only a lad, my Donald."

She pursed her lips tightly and took a sip of tea.

Someone to talk to, Alice thought. At last!

"You must miss him terribly," she said.

Mrs. Belmore looked away as she smoked and said nothing.

"I was wondering," Alice ventured, "about Captain Bramwell ..."

"Ah!" Mrs. Belmore, exclaimed as she stood. "Thought you'd catch me off my guard, did ya? The old cow would hang me out to dry if she knew we was talkin' about the Cap'n, so you can just clear off!"

Alice didn't want to let her go that quickly.

"Is the food still disappearing?" she asked hastily.

" 'Tis," Mrs. Belmore confirmed. "Here and there, now an' then, an' it ain't no one from the village would come all the way up here for a can of beans. Doesn't make sense, does it? I even have to be careful not to leave me fags in the kitchen. They'll be gone by mornin' sure as yer standin'."

She waved the girl off, stamped out her cigarette and turned to go back into the house.

"Who or what's been sneakin' 'round has me at wit's end," she said as she went through the door. "Gives me the creeps!"

Alice was mutually ill at ease, but relieved to learn that the blame had been lifted from her.

She spent the first part of the afternoon exploring the grounds about the house and was disappointed to find the stables were empty of livestock. She would have loved to have a horse to converse with. The garage was large enough for a single automobile, but the car was in use by Mrs. Thorndike in the village. Alice idly resumed her exploration but found herself continually drawn back to the footpath that led to the Captain's cottage. Eventually she was compelled to yield to her curiosity as she set forth on the trail as if pulled by a magnetic force, staying alert to the possibility that she might encounter the Captain somewhere along the way.

Soon she was beside the lake, and she stopped there, hoping to pass her time watching the birds and waterfowl in and around its surface. She decided that the most convenient spot to pursue that activity would be from the gazebo, and though she still sensed a ghostly air about the location, she summoned her courage and managed her way through the overgrowth of vegetation and in a short time she stood in the middle of the structure.

Brushing aside the dead leaves that cluttered the surface of one of the chairs, Alice settled herself in one of them. As she sat, she found the tranquility of the view before her almost hypnotic, and gradually the tension she had felt when she approached the gazebo drained from her body. Presently her head fell gently and slowly to the side as she drifted into sleep.

Alice had not slept long before the sound of a dog's bark drifted across from the opposite side of the lake. At first it did not arouse her, but as the sound was repeated, it finally struck her, and she was startled awake, her eyes wide with excitement. Jumping to her feet, she strained her eyes trying to bring into focus the figures she could only barely discern on the opposite shore.

The shade of a heavy growth of trees at the edge of the lake cast a dimness over the water's edge, but eventually Alice was able to make out two figures. Banner, continually barking in her direction, was standing next to Captain Bramwell, whose head and face, save for his left eye, was again wrapped in a black scarf.

Banner ran about excitedly, only pausing a moment before the Captain, as if asking permission to be dismissed. Alice could see the man nod his head in approval, and the dog was away in an instant. Her heart nearly burst with excitement.

She made her way through the underbrush to the smooth, sandy edge of the lake and was there when Banner rounded the curve of the shore, barking wildly as he rushed to her. She wrapped her arms around him as he leapt up to her, pushing her backward onto the sand, where he laid on her chest, wagging his tail and licking her face in a frenzy as she laughed. She was sure Banner was laughing too, and the two of them wrestled happily. He opened his mouth wide and made a playful half bark, half moaning sound, but was careful not to accidentally harm her with his teeth as he frolicked.

Alice chided him for not visiting her room after the first night.

"I'm sorry I haven't been able to get a new ball for you as of yet," she said to him. "I hope you're not too disappointed, but I'll find one for you soon enough. Somehow I will, I promise. Now, where is your old ball? Did you bring it with you? How can we play fetch if you don't have your ball?"

The dog cocked his head to the side.

"Well, no matter. We'll find something else. I know! A stick!"

Alice pushed Banner off her chest and stood. Looking across the lake she could see the Captain, watching the two of them interact. She stood for a moment looking back at him and then smiled and waved tenuously. At first there was no response, as he stood stone still. Finally, however, slightly and almost imperceptibly, he raised his left-hand palm up to return her greeting, as he leaned against his crutch to maintain his balance.

She didn't know if he could see her smile across the distance between them, but she hoped he sensed it. She figured someone in his condition could do with a good smile now and then.

Banner's bark brought her attention back to the matter at hand, and she started a search through the brush that grew unkempt and neglected about the area, looking for a proper stick. It didn't take long to find one, and she held it up for Banner to inspect.

"What do you think, boy?" she asked the dog. "Will this do? Give it a try!"

Banner caught on immediately, and he barked and began a couple of false starts in anticipation of her toss. Alice hurled the stick a good distance, and the collie rushed after it with lightning speed, then promptly returned with it, prancing proudly as he dropped it at her feet. She praised him highly and with a mighty heave, tossed it again, a little farther than the last, sending it into a pile of shrubbery. Banner bolted toward it in quick pursuit.

Swiftly reaching the vicinity where the stick had landed, the dog began searching for it amid the debris, unable at first to locate it. There was a good deal of sniffing about, and he poked his nose into the vines in various places as he searched for his treasure.

"I'm sorry, boy!" Alice called to him. "I didn't mean to lose it. You'll find it, though. Come on, keep searching. It's there somewhere!"

At length, Banner reached into a pile of ivy and grabbed a twig that was similar in size to the stick Alice had thrown. The ivy was tightly wrapped around it and clung fast requiring considerable effort to wrestle it free from its grip but at last he succeeded in extricating it. He rushed back with his prize, with some of the vine still clinging tightly to the twig.

"No, silly" Alice said as she picked it up and examined it after he dropped it at her feet. "This isn't the right stick. This will never do."

She disposed of the twig by turning and throwing it into the distance behind her, intending to direct Banner back in the direction she had thrown the first stick, but he misunderstood and chased after the rejected object.

"No, Banner!" she shouted to him. "Not that one! Leave it! Come back here!"

Banner had already grabbed the twig and was rushing back to her before she even finished yelling her order to him. She laughed as he delivered it to her, sitting before it, barking and wagging his tail enthusiastically as if demanding she toss it again.

"You're not a very good listener, you know," she said

and she teasingly waved the twig in front of him as he snapped at it. "Let's just get rid of this."

In her home neighborhood, Alice was known to all the playmates her age for possessing the ability to throw a ball farther than any of them. That pitch enabled her to throw Banner's unwanted stick far across the surface of the lake, where it lay floating near a thicket of ivy and reeds that sprung up through the water.

Intending to chase after the stick, Banner rushed to the water's edge and stopped, rushing back and forth in confusion.

"No, Banner! Here!" Alice yelled, but his attention could not be diverted from the discarded twig, and he ignored her.

Alice was startled as she watched Banner suddenly decide to enter the water. He waded in as far as he could touch bottom, and then began swimming, heading toward the reeds. She called him back, but her commands fell on deaf ears.

Pulling off her shoes and stockings, she rushed into the lake, only entering far enough for the water to still reach her knees. She could feel her feet sink into the deep, slimy mud. On the far shore, she could see the Captain limping as fast as he was able, circling around the edge of the water toward her.

At first Banner was able to paddle smoothly to the spot where the twig lay floating near the reeds and he snatched it up, but he inhaled a mouthful of water in the process that momentarily gagged him, and he began hacking up water as he turned to head back to shore. Suddenly he began splashing frantically with his front feet. Alice promptly recognized what was happening. He had apparently managed to get one of his hind legs tangled in the vines that grew among the reeds and was unable to break free.

Screaming his name, Alice rushed about trying to figure out what she could do to help him before he drowned, but she didn't know how to swim, and she began crying hysterically. A sudden memory flashed across her mind, and she looked around the shore until she spotted the small, decrepit rowboat she had seen earlier. Racing toward it, she began desperately dislodging it from the weeds that covered it. Time and weather had caused the skiff to be imbedded in the sand, but rocking it back and forth and lifting it above the line of sand that surrounded it, she was able to extricate it from its confinement. With all the strength she could muster, she was finally able to push it toward the water.

She could hear Banner splashing loudly as he struggled to keep his head above water, and Alice knew she must lose no time in getting to him before he became too tired to tread water. That thought spurred her on, and with a mighty shove she launched the boat into the water and jumped in. She was relieved to find the remains of a paddle on the mud-covered floor of the boat and though it had been broken in half, it was enough for her to manage to propel her on the water and she rowed madly. Alice had never rowed a boat before, so it took her several attempts before she finally figured out the best method for navigating it as it veered from side to side.

It didn't take long for her to notice that a large hole existed underneath the layer of mud at her feet as water began freely bubbling up from beneath and quickly began filling the craft. In her eagerness to save Banner, she gave no thought to the danger that now threatened her as she strenuously continued rowing toward him.

By the time she reached his side, the boat was more than half submerged. Nevertheless, she was hopeful that she could rescue the dog and return to shore before it completely sank. Banner scratched at the side of the skiff as she drew near, and she leaned over its edge to reach his hind feet to locate the vine that constrained him. She discovered that only one leg was tangled, and using both hands, she pulled at the vine with all her might. It took two attempts before she was able to untamgle it.

Banner was trying to climb aboard the boat with Alice, and she wrapped her arms around him, just behind his neck and tried to help him. The weight of the girl and the dog, however, capsized the boat and it was quickly engulfed in water as it began sinking. One side of it remained above water long enough for her to grab on to it a moment to catch her breath, and she held tight with one hand, while using the other to steady Banner, who was also clinging to the side of the boat with his front feet as he panted and coughed up water.

The boat gradually began its descent, leaving Alice in a panic as she wildly tried to figure out how she could get back to shore. There were no pieces of wood floating anywhere, nor could she locate any other means of keeping herself afloat. Soon she was out of time, and the boat sank below the water leaving her frantically thrashing about.

Banner had gotten just enough rest to restore his strength, and he started swimming back to the shore.

"Help!" Alice screamed after him. "Help me, Banner!"

From the shore, the Captain had helplessly witnessed the entire event, physically unable to provide any assistance. As the dog neared the shore, however, he began waving him back.

"Go back, Banner!" he called out to him, his voice muffled behind his scarf. "You must go back! Help her, Banner! Help the girl!"

As Banner paddled his way to the bank of the river, he acknowledged the command, and soon he had turned himself around and headed back toward Alice.

She was fighting hard to keep her head above water by moving her arms up and down and kicking her legs, but the effort had little effect and served only to exhaust her. Her face was turned upward to the sky, but she wasn't able to hold her head up far enough to prevent water from continuing to flood her mouth. From where he stood, the Captain could see that the lake would very soon swallow Alice if Banner failed to rescue her.

Seeming to glide across the surface of the water, the dog soon drew near and circled her.

"His tail!" the Captain bellowed. "Grab his tail! He'll pull you ashore!"

Reacting to the command, Alice reached for Banner's tail as he completed his circle around her and began heading back for dry land. The added weight pulled him down and slowed him considerably, but he pushed on with tenacity and determination, drawing from what little strength remained in his body. Alice held to him tightly, making every effort to hold her head up as he struggled to tow her behind. The closer Banner drew to shore, the slower he travelled, and he coughed continually as water repeatedly filled his throat.

For what seemed an eternity to the Captain, he watched

Banner's heroic efforts with despair, cursing the fates for preventing him from being of any help. It was only through sheer stouteheartedness that the collie was at last close enough to the point where the muddy floor of the lake rose to meet the shore. When Alice's feet could at last touch the murky bottom, she released Banner's tail, sinking to her knees as she struggled to pull herself out of the water. Banner reached land first and turned to make sure she was safe before vigorously shaking off the water from his fur.

On her hands and knees, Alice dragged herself onto the shore, and when she was clear of the water, she lay coughing and gasping for breath. Banner shook himself again and sniffed her face as his tail wagged.

The Captain managed to stand before her, his body shaking with anger.

"What in God's name were you thinking?" he screamed at her, his voice cracking. "What made you think Banner could swim? And what did you hope to accomplish in that ancient wreck of a boat? You and Banner could both have drowned, you brainless, half-wit! You deserve to drown, but not *him*! Not Banner!"

He managed to lift his crutch, as if to strike her with it, but he lost his balance and had to lean against it to prevent from falling.

"I didn't mean for him to …," Alice tried to respond in a raspy voice.

The Captain turned away from her and started to hobble away, then stopped and turned back to her to continue his tirade.

"What was I thinking? I was prepared to start admitting

him back into the house at night to keep you company. I would have to be crazy to allow you anywhere near him again! Don't you dare come back here, do you understand? Stay as far away as you can from me and from Banner, you worthless little imbecile!"

He was about to say more, but instead he uttered an exasperated growl, turned and headed back to his cottage.

"Come, Banner! Come!" he commanded the dog angrily.

The collie, water still dripping from his coat, looked down at Alice and whined, wishing he could remain by her side, but when the Captain called him again, he turned slowly, and with his tail held low between his legs, walked reluctantly and pitifully after him.

CHAPTER SIX

Sunday morning Mrs. Thorndike entered Alice's room without knocking, as usual.

"Time for breakfast," she said as she hung a new dress in the wardrobe and drew wide the curtains, admitting a bright ray of sunshine that fell directly onto Alice' face. "We shall be attending church this morning, and we will not be late, so don't dawdle."

Alice yawned, rubbed her eyes and stretched her arms.

"Oh, yes," Mrs. Thorndike said as she paused at the doorway before exiting. "We shall wait until this afternoon to discuss your outrageous activities yesterday. Dragging yourself through the mud? I have no idea what you thought you were doing, but since this is Sunday and we will be attending services, we'll postpone discussion until later. While you're in God's house, you would do well to ask His forgiveness for whatever nonsense you've been up to."

Alice was relieved that at least Mrs. Thorndike didn't know about the details of the incident at the lake, so she figured she'd better start making up a story and hope the Captain wouldn't confide in her. When she had gotten back to the house the previous day, she had quickly thrown her wet, muddy clothes in a pile on the floor and then cleaned herself up, but Anna had discovered them before Alice had a chance to hide them. With a gasp and a shocked look in the girl's direction, the maid gathered up the clothes in a sheet and hauled them away without saying a word. Alice had spent the night wondering what repercussions she would face.

The drive to the village was only a 20-minute journey with Ridley behind the wheel, and Mrs. Thorndike next to him. Alice, in her new dress and shoes, sat uncomfortably between Anna and Mrs. Belmore, who smelled strongly of cigarettes. It came as no surprise to Alice that the trip was made in silence. She wanted to strike up a conversation with Mrs. Belmore but when she caught a glimpse of Mrs. Thorndike's eyes staring back at her with disfavor through the side mirror, she reconsidered.

The village was small and looked as if it might not have seen any changes in well over a century, other than a recently graded field that ran by the schoolhouse on the edge of the community. Once intended for military use, the field was later abandoned. There were scarcely any shops; a butcher, bakery and a merchant who sold general merchandise were the few she caught sight of. Her biggest disappointments were the absence of a bookstore and cinema. It occurred to Alice that the village might be just as dull as the house Mrs. Thorndike ran.

As they pulled up before the church, Mrs. Thorndike turned to Alice as the others exited.

"Now, remember," she said, "avoid conversation with these people other than a simple 'hello' or 'good morning.' What goes on at the Captain's estate is none of their concern."

Alice nodded her understanding but decided that whatever conversation she chose to engage in was none of Mrs. Thorndike's concern either.

As she moved to get out of the car, Mrs. Thorndike noticed that she was wearing her blue scarf around her neck. She reached for it.

"That rag doesn't match your outfit," Alice was told.

"Leave it in the car."

She opened her mouth to protest, but Mrs. Thorndike had already brusquely tossed it aside.

From the moment Alice entered the church, she was the source of great curiosity as the villagers watched her, some attempting to conceal their inquisitiveness, others less so. The children, in particular, nudged one another and whispered in each other's ears as their parents reprimanded them with nudges and stern frowns. They empathized with their children's interest, but there was a certain decorum that had to be maintained in a house of prayer.

Mrs. Thorndike selected a seating location for the household as near as possible to the rear of the church, which resulted in many craned necks among those seated in front.

The contents of the young vicar's sermon that morning failed to match the enthusiasm of his delivery and bored Alice into a daydream in which she and the Captain's grand collie frolicked in the sunshine over gently rolling hills covered in flowers of every color. She forgot all sense of time and place, and when the service was at last concluded, she was startled back to consciousness by the sound of everyone's making his or her way through the pews.

Mrs. Thorndike had hoped to hasten Alice back to the car but was stopped by the vicar, who greeted her warmly.

"You appear to be in a bit of a rush this morning, Missus Thorndike," he said. "I hope Captain Bramwell hasn't been making too many demands of you on Sundays. Aren't you going to introduce me to your new lodger?"

"Of course," she replied. "This is Miss Alice Piper. She's Doctor Finlay's charge. She's an evacuee from Coventry and she'll be in our care until her father returns from the front."

"Ah yes," he said as he shook Alice's hand. A group of churchgoers had started to assemble near them, trying to make it appear that they wanted to greet the vicar, but in reality, they wanted to learn about the new girl. "Doctor Finlay visited me when he drove you here a few days ago. He asked me to check in on you from time to time."

"Of course," Mrs. Thorndike responded nervously. "Please be certain to give us a ring before you drop in, won't you? We must respect the Captain's privacy."

She started to move away, but the vicar grabbed her arm.

"Oh, I mustn't forget," he said, looking around among the people gathered outside. "The curate wanted a word."

Spotting an elderly gentleman, he waved him over. "Mayor Applebee, a moment if you please!"

The man smiled and waved back and approached them. Mrs. Thorndike grimaced and bent down to Alice, whispering in her ear, "Straight to the car and wait for me there."

It was apparent to Alice that the curate's discussion with Mrs. Thorndike would be anything but brief, so she was relieved to be excused. She would have obeyed, too, had her attention not first been drawn toward the churchyard. Inscriptions on tombstones always held a peculiar fascination for her, and she seldom passed up the opportunity for a visitation. As she strolled among them this time, however, she found herself in a different state of mind. This time she was overcome with sadness, and after reading the inscription upon one particular gravestone, she realised why.

Mary Ann Canfield
Beloved Mother and Wife
1880 - 1914

As she stood before the woman's grave she felt as if she were standing by her mother's final resting place in Coventry, for she had died at the same age. She knew that if she were there again she would still feel just as lonely, but she thought that being near her once more might give her some sense of comfort. She was considering searching for a flower to place upon the mother's grave when a female voice spoke to her from behind.

"Hello, there."

Alice turned to see an attractive, blonde-haired woman in her mid 40's, of whom she was not aware had followed her. The woman had apparently come from the church and now stood before her, with a pleasant smile, clutching a small handbag.

"Was Missus Canfield someone you knew?" the lady asked, nodding to the grave marker.

"No, ma'am," Alice answered shyly. "I was just … well, you see, my mother died at the same age as this lady."

"Oh, I see," the lady said in a comforting voice. "I'm Missus Richardson. I teach school here in the village. I was told all about you. Word travels quite fast in a community this small, you see. I'm so very sorry about your mother. I'm sure it hasn't been at all easy for you. How are you holding up, my dear?"

Alice shrugged.

"How has Missus Thorndike been treating you?" the lady asked. "Has she been helping you with your lessons?"

"She told me she will," Alice replied. "So far she's only given me textbooks to read."

"I do hope she follows through," Mrs. Richardson said, nodding with a concerned look on her face. "We had hoped you would join us in my classroom here in the village. We don't understand why you aren't allowed."

Alice shrugged again.

"And Captain Bramwell," the teacher began, "has he ...?"

Suddenly Mrs. Thorndike's commanding voice interrupted their discussion as she called Alice from nearby.

"What on earth are you doing here, girl? I've been searching for you! I thought I told you to go straight to the car and to wait for me there."

"Yes, ma'am," Alice answered meekly as she moved to join her.

"We were just getting to know one another, Missus Thorndike," Mrs. Richardson said. "Must she leave so soon?"

"Yes, I'm afraid she must," Mrs. Thorndike answered curtly as she turned to escort Alice back to the car.

Mrs. Richardson attempted to catch up with them. "I was hoping Alice might accept my invitation to join me for tea. If not today, sometime soon. My son and husband are away right now, you know, and I would so much enjoy getting to know ..."

Mrs. Thorndike stopped abruptly.

"I'm afraid that would be quite out of the question, Missus Richardson," she said, glaring angrily at her. "I'm sure Captain Bramwell would not approve. He would not wish her to have anything to do with you. *You* of *all* people!"

Mrs. Thorndike hastened toward the car clutching Alice's arm tightly, leaving behind the schoolteacher, who was too shocked by the anger in the housekeeper's voice to respond.

Approaching the car, where Mrs. Belmore and Anna were seated in back and Ridley sat in front behind the wheel, they were greeted by a man in his mid-60's, who opened the front passenger door for Mrs. Thorndike. His upper lip was completely engulfed in a thick, gray moustache and he was attired in a Home Guard uniform that was composed of loose-fitting khaki-colored denim overalls, a field service cap and an armband bearing the initials "L. D. V.," which identified him as a Local Defence Volunteer. He took his responsibility seriously.

"Missus Thorndike, if I may," he said as he stood beside the door. "I wonder if I might have a word."

"Not today, Mister Phipps," she replied with boredom in her voice as she climbed into the car and Alice stepped into the back.

"Ah," he corrected her, pointing to an insignia on the top of his shoulder, "that's *Sergeant* Phipps now, if you please, Missus Thorndike, of the L.D.V., and I'm afraid I must insist."

"What do you want?" she said with a deep sigh speaking to him through the open window as Ridley started the car.

"Well, you see," Phipps said, trying to sound as officious as possible, "I've been receiving reports from my superior officers to be on the lookout for any mysterious activity in the area, and it occurred to me if Captain Bramwell, being a fellow veteran of the Great War and all, might make himself available for a brief discussion, we might …"

"No. Thank you," Mrs. Thorndike replied dismissively as she cranked her window closed and nodded for Ridley to drive on.

Mrs. Thorndike didn't pass up the opportunity to glare at Alice as they sat down to supper that afternoon. Alice was not in a mood to care, and her indifference was well-noted.

"Finish your supper quickly," Mrs. Thorndike said. "When you have finished, you may wait for me in the study. I will address your misbehaviour there." She seemed to be looking forward to the reprimand.

Alice did not respond.

At that moment, Ridley entered the kitchen, looking officious as usual.

"You're late, Mister Ridley," Mrs. Thorndike pointed out.

"I'm afraid it couldn't be helped, ma'am," he responded. "I've been tending to Captain Bramwell, and he asked me to wait until he had finished composing a letter. He instructed me to deliver it to Miss Piper."

The butler handed an envelope to Alice. Her name was typewritten across the front, and she stared at it in disbelief, hesitating to accept it.

"I'll take that, if you please," Mrs. Thorndike commanded, extending her hand.

Ridley held the envelope back from her.

"Captain Bramwell was most emphatic," he told her. "I have been instructed to deliver the message to Miss Piper alone and to no one else."

Mrs. Thorndike reacted with a slight gasp of disbelief, and Ridley once again extended the envelope to Alice, who accepted it with apprehension. The butler seated himself at the table, and Alice timidly started to unseal the message until she noticed that everyone's attention was focused on her.

"May I be excused to go to my room?" Alice asked. "I should like to read my letter in private, if you please."

Mrs. Thorndike looked away from her and gave her a slight, reluctant nod.

Alice took the steps two at a time as she eagerly made her way to her room. Seating herself on the edge of her bed, she tore open the envelope. Her hands were shaking as she read the typewritten letter.

Dear Miss Piper

It is with deepest shame that I compose this letter to you for the purpose of begging your forgiveness for the outrageously shameful behaviour to which I subjected you during our previous meetings. You were totally undeserving of such treatment, and I am filled with deepest remorse.

I most sincerely pray you can find it in your heart to forgive me. As you have probably already been told, I suffer greatly with horrific pain, both physical and emotional, sustained during the last war, which often brings about uncontrollable behaviour, as you have witnessed.

I offer this explanation so that you will understand my actions, not because I expect to be excused from blame. An apology is meaningless if one believes unacceptable conduct was justified.

Please accept my invitation to join Banner and me for

afternoon tea at our cottage today at 3:00.

I very much look forward to making your acquaintance and learning what we can do to make your stay with us a pleasant experience during what must be a very difficult time for you.

Sincerely,

Joshua Bramwell

Alice reread the letter several times. Had such an invitation ever been extended to anyone else during the many years the Captain had lived alone? Had he ever before humbled himself with such an apology, she wondered. She was filled with excitement at the prospect of meeting with him, but she promised herself she would not let him detect her nervousness. With Banner by her side, she knew she would find courage.

She lifted a corner of the carpet and shoved the letter beneath, expecting Mrs. Thorndike to search her room for it later. Although Alice didn't think the note contained any secrets, she relished the thought of teasing the housekeeper by making her think there were, and she smiled as she strolled down the stairs to the study with an air of self-confidence.

Alice found the study unoccupied so she scanned the bookshelves while she waited for Mrs. Thorndike's arrival. They were all quite old and though most dealt with issues of farm management, animal husbandry, theology and political philosophy, she continued to scan the titles in the hope of finding something that might be of interest to an 11-year-old reader.

"You'll find nothing there for a child of your age," Mrs.

Thorndike assured her as she entered the room and seated herself behind the desk.

"How am I to advance my education if I only read books intended for 11-year-olds?" Alice countered.

"You're impertinent as well as foolish," Mrs. Thorndike responded. "You're a child, and your small little brain has not yet advanced to a level that could understand what is contained in those books, if it ever will."

"Have you read any of them?" Alice asked.

Mrs. Thorndike indicated the chair in front of her desk.

"There are those who might judge someone such as you as precocious," Mrs. Thorndike said as Alice seated herself. "I'm not one of them. Now, to the matter at hand …"

She stopped as she noticed Alice's dress.

"Why are you still dressed for Sunday services? When I've finished with you, go up to your room and put on one of those dreadful garments you brought with you. You mustn't ruin the one decent dress you have by crawling in the mud or something equally daft."

Alice examined her dress with mock surprise.

"Oh, but don't you think this would be far more appropriate dress to wear when I meet with Captain Bramwell?'

Mrs. Thorndike's eyes and mouth widened with amazement. Alice pretended to be surprised and placed her hand over her mouth as she gasped.

"Oh, dear!" she said condescendingly. "Didn't he inform you that I am to join him for tea this afternoon?"

Alice furrowed her brow and appeared concerned.

"Surely you'll be joining us?" she asked. "Oh, silly me. I forgot! It would hardly be proper for a member of staff to be invited to tea with the master of the house, would it?"

"I don't know how this has come about," Mrs. Thorndike said, regaining her authority and sitting up straight and stiff. "In 26 years, Captain Bramwell has never, not *once* met socially with anyone save Doctor Finlay. You heed my words: You are to conduct yourself with grace and maturity, do you understand?"

"Well, I shall certainly do my very best, Missus Thorndike," Alice said with fake innocence, "but it may be difficult for a child my age. After all, you know, my 'small little brain' may not have yet advanced to a level that could understand how to behave in such circumstances."

Mrs. Thorndike stood, shaking with rage and pointed a finger at Alice.

"You shall pay for your impudence!" she declared. "You'll very soon learn I am not to be crossed!"

"I understand, Missus Thorndike," Alice said calmly as she walked to the door and then paused. "I'll be certain to convey your words to Captain Bramwell. I'm certain he will be pleased to know you have everything well under control."

Closing the door behind her, she heard a loud "thump" as Mrs. Thorndike hurled something solid at the other side. Alice had taught herself a lesson that she would use to her advantage throughout the rest of her life. Remaining calm and restrained in the face of unreasonable anger is the only way to maintain control over an aggressor.

At three o'clock sharp, Alice stood before the Captain's dwelling and knocked on the front door. The sound drew an immediate response from Banner, who ran from behind the cottage barking and happily wagging his tail as he rounded the corner and eagerly greeted Alice. She knelt and roughed his fur as she hugged him.

"Back here, if you please!" she heard the Captain's voice call out from the back, and she followed Banner as he led her to him.

She found Captain Bramwell standing in the same spot she had first seen him. His head and face were draped behind his familiar black scarf, and, as before, he was staring into the forest, as if watching for something hiding from him there.

"Ah!" he said and approached her with difficulty, stopping to extend his one good left hand in greeting. "Allow me to formally and properly introduce myself. I am Joshua Bramwell, often referred to as 'the Captain,' though I, myself, am not fond of the title."

For the brief moment he held her hand, she found his grip weak and trembling. His words were slurred, and he spoke with a slight lisp.

"I thought you might enjoy your tea out here on the lawn," he said, nodding toward a table and two chairs that had been placed there. "Ridley will be here shortly with the refreshments."

He escorted her to the table and nodded toward one of the chairs.

"I hope you'll forgive me," he apologized, "I'm unable to assist you with your chair, as you can see."

"That's not at all necessary," Alice said as she seated herself. "In fact, I've learned to be quite independent."

The Captain awkwardly pulled his chair back from the

table and sat himself.

His bearing was far from what Alice had expected from someone who was regarded with both fear and respect and who, as a military officer, had once commanded men in combat. He seemed meek and unsure of himself. Seated across from her, he started several times to speak, but in his discomfort, he was unable to find the words.

Banner sat close by her side and placed his head in her lap.

"No, Banner," the Captain said with a stutter. "You mustn't …"

"Oh, that's quite all right," Alice assured him as she stroked Banner's head. "I love having him near me. He's very comforting, wouldn't you agree?"

The Captain agreed with a slight nod.

"He was a gift from Doctor Finlay," he told her. As he spoke of the dog he became visibly more relaxed and comfortable. "Several years ago, I became quite … depressed. Depression is a condition that plagues me constantly, but there came a time in my life when I had fallen to a depth from which I believed I would never recover. I was determined to take my own life.

"Then on the very day I had planned my own execution, I heard a sound at my front door. When I opened it, I found, looking up at me with all the innocence of the world, that young, incredible little collie. Nearby I found a package of dog food, a dish and a note from Doctor Finlay in which he lectured me for being so pitifully self-absorbed and so damned sensitive. He said I needed someone with whom I could share the love he was certain still lurked somewhere deep within me and that if I could bring myself to manage even just a wee bit of affection toward the fellow on my front doorstep, that affection would be returned beyond measure. He placed the responsibility for the well-being of that mischievous, playful little soul into my care. He knew Missus Thorndike would never come near him and would likely forbid the staff to stay away as well. Doctor Finlay was right, as usual. I have grown to love Banner as I can love no other."

Banner had closed his eyes as his head lay in Alice's lap while she petted him, but her chair was pulled back enough from the table to enable the dog to see his master nearby and when he heard his name spoken, he looked toward the Captain before gradually and contentedly closing his eyes again.

"That dog," the Captain continued, "that incredible creature, forgives me even when I am overtaken by one of my uncontrollable rages. He holds no grudge for even my most unforgivable behaviour, and at the end of every day since he has been delivered into my care, he lays his head upon my lap as I sit before the fireplace and gazes into this wretched, ghastly face of mine with an expression of absolute adoration and devotion as if he were looking upon the most beautiful, exquisite face in the world. That expression speaks to me, and it says, 'I would do *anything* for you,' and he asks for nothing in return, nothing but to be near me. I don't know what I would do without him."

He turned silent again. Alice was totally unprepared for the suddenness of such a candid confession. Could this be the same man who had screamed at her in their previous encounter?

Realizing that Banner was a good inducement to get him to open up, she asked, "How did you come to name him 'Banner'?"

"There was a young Scotsman in my regiment," the Captain told her as he looked down at the ground, "and he was nicknamed 'Banner.' I don't know how he came by it. He endured a great deal of teasing from all of the men, but he knew they were all playing with him because we all loved him dearly. He died, of course, along with my brother and everyone else under my command. I was the only one to survive, if you can call my condition 'surviving.'"

He shifted his body with some discomfort.

"I would prefer not to talk about it, if you don't mind," he said.

Alice tried to think of another topic to cheer him.

"You have an awful lot of books," she declared.

"Indeed," he agreed. "Other than Banner, they are my only source of pleasure."

"Are they from the library in the large house?" she asked.

"Those? Oh heavens, no. Those were my father's books. I doubt there would be anything there of interest to you. Hasn't Missus Thorndike provided you with any books?"

"Only textbooks."

"Then you must look through my library. I'm sure you'll find many books that will interest you there. I can think of several titles I think you would enjoy."

Alice was eager to learn what books he had in mind, but at that moment Ridley arrived, pushing a tea cart.

"I apologize for my tardiness, sir," he said as he placed a setting before Alice, which aroused Banner's curiosity.

"Were you detained by Missus Thorndike by chance?" the Captain asked.

"I'm afraid so, sir." Ridley replied.

"Ah!" Captain Bramwell exclaimed knowingly. "I'm not surprised. I'll have a word with her."

"If it isn't asking too much, sir, I would much rather you didn't. I'm sure you will appreciate that when she believes she has received a reprimand she can make things rather difficult for the rest of us."

"Leave it to me, Ridley," the Captain reassured him.

"Sugar and cream, Miss?" Ridley asked Alice, removing the lid from the sugar bowl.

"Yes, please," Alice started to say. "Three spoons of …"

She noticed that only one setting had been placed on the table, and she was the only one being served.

"Where is Captain Bramwell's tea?"

"I won't be having any, I'm afraid," the Captain replied. "Please forgive me."

"Why on earth not?" Alice asked.

"You were invited to tea and you have been served. I'm under no obligation to partake."

"Is it bad for your health?"

The Captain was becoming slightly agitated.

"No. Let's just leave it at that, shall we?"

"But I can't …," Alice started to say.

"Don't be foolish, young lady," he interrupted, and

began to tremble slightly. "Very well, if you must know, I would not subject you to the gore that lurks behind this scarf. Not now, at tea, not any time. You would be repulsed, and the sight would turn an otherwise pleasant and enjoyable occasion into a stomach-turning nightmare. Please leave it and enjoy your tea."

Alice pushed her serving away.

"Thank you, Ridley," she said to the butler. "If Captain Bramwell isn't having tea today, then neither shall I."

The butler looked toward Captain Bramwell who nodded in response.

"Very well, Miss," Ridley replied as he collected the service and then departed.

"I know you are very young and very wise beyond your years" the Captain said, trying to control his irritation, "but I beg you to understand. I have chosen to live alone for 26 years because I cannot bear the thought of others being repulsed by the sight of me, nor can I tolerate their pity. The war left me not only visibly and emotionally scarred, but the gas attacks I endured ravaged my nervous system, and the lingering effects subject me to unexpected and uncontrollable fits of rage. At your tender age you cannot begin to imagine the horrors I have endured, to see my brother ... to see someone you love, alive and vibrant one second and in the next blown to pieces before your eyes. I don't need ..."

Alice bristled and was about to contradict his words when the Captain's attention was suddenly distracted, and he promptly stopped talking. He knocked his chair backward as he suddenly stood and leaned heavily on his crutch as his one, uncovered eye darted about the edge of the forest. The unexpected abruptness of his actions and the fear his behaviour conveyed scared her.

"There!" he whispered eerily as he pointed toward the woods. "Did you see it? It's out there. It's watching us!"

As Alice tried desperately to understand what had so suddenly possessed him, Banner took off like a shot in the direction the Captain pointed, barking frantically.

"No, Banner, NO!" Captain Bramwell yelled. "Come back here. Come!"

Banner stopped before reaching the edge of the forest but continued barking.

"What is it?" Alice asked desperately. "What do you see out there?"

"I'm sorry if I frightened you, Miss Piper," he replied, breathing heavily, "but you must know and you must believe me. There is something out there, deep within that forest. It's an evil thing that watches us and waits. It waits for the opportunity to sneak up on us at night to murder us in our beds!

He turned to Alice and held out his hand to her.

"You must believe me. Please! No one else will believe me. Only Banner and I know it exists, and someone must stop it before it's too late!"

"A wolf, perhaps," Alice offered.

"Ah!" he said, waving the idea aside. "Wolves were hunted to extinction from this forest before my father was born. It is no mere wolf."

He turned back to the forest and was silent for a moment. Banner was still barking.

"Come here!" he called out to the dog. "Come back now! Come quickly! You mustn't get too close!"

Banner reluctantly turned and began walking back toward the Captain, his head held low.

"Get away from here now, Miss Piper," he said desperately. "Run back to the house and tell the staff what you have seen. Tell them it won't wait much longer. It will come for us soon. Run! Quickly!"

Alice ran as fast as she could. She had seen nothing, but Captain Bramwell had convinced her. There was something truly terrifying and unspeakable waiting beyond the edge of the forest.

CHAPTER SEVEN

Alice rushed frantically about the house searching for Mrs.Thorndike before eventually finding her in the drawing room seated before a front window reading a newspaper and having tea.

"Missus Thorndike!" Alice exclaimed breathlessly as she stood next to her. "You must come quickly. Captain Bramwell says we are all in great danger. There's something in the woods ..."

Mrs. Thorndike continued reading her newspaper for a moment before calmly setting it down. She took a sip of tea and removed her reading glasses before looking up.

"My dear child," she said with a slight smile, "there is nothing of the sort."

"But Captain Bramwell ... Banner ...," Alice struggled to say.

"Captain Bramwell is only having another of his hallucinations. He suffers from severe mental trauma brought about by the lingering effects of the war. I have known him for far longer than you, and I can assure you, we are in no danger. He has been imagining these fantasies for several weeks now, and I regret that his mental condition seems to be worsening."

Alice was not convinced, but Mrs. Thorndike shook her head with an attitude that spoke of arrogance and conceit.

"Now run along. There is no ogre in our forest."

Mrs. Thorndike put her glasses back on and resumed reading her newspaper.

Alice could see she was getting nowhere so she ran to

the kitchen to find Mrs. Belmore. She found her seated at the kitchen table with Ridley and Anna, who took the news with indifference.

"But even if you don't believe the Captain, you can't think Banner is hallucinating as well," Alice said, baffled.

"Banner?" Mrs. Belmore questioned with a laugh. "That's your authority, is it? That animal wouldn't know the difference between a hobgoblin and a squirrel!"

Ridley and Anna laughed with her, and Alice turned away, dejected, and returned to her room. She remained convinced of the Captain's vision, and she continued to feel uneasy throughout dinner later that evening and well past bedtime.

Though she couldn't stop thinking about Captain Bramwell's distressful warning, she hadn't forgotten the words he declared just before he was distracted by the specter in the forest, and they continued to simmer inside her.

"... At your tender age you cannot imagine ... To see someone you love, alive and vibrant one second, and in the next blown to pieces before your eyes ..."

How could he know, she thought angrily? He really knew very little about her and what she had experienced before she arrived at his home. Now his words brought back the most dreadful day in her life and left her downhearted. The memory of that event weighed heavily upon her and re-enacted itself in her dreams as she finally drifted to sleep.

She remembered the morning the bombing had stopped, leaving her shivering with cold and fear in the basement near her home where she had sought shelter. Her mother had been working at the hospital for the last two days, and Alice knew from previous bombings that she would probably be there for several nights more, so she was on her own, huddling with neighbors and school friends in the cramped darkness.

When the "all clear" siren had sounded, Alice stumbled from the shelter into the morning air, thick with smoke and the smell of gas and many other nauseating odors. She was only one block from the little house where she lived with her mother and father, but it was difficult to find her way because all of the familiar landmarks she would normally use to guide her on her way home were nowhere to be seen. The streets were running with water and people everywhere were bandaged or were bandaging the wounded, while many others were digging through the rubble, some with their bare hands, to help those who had been buried in their homes. Those who were not so occupied were shuffling through the ruins in a daze, shell-shocked, not knowing if they were coming or going. There were bodies lying about, some covered with sheets while others still lay exposed, unmoving, contorted in awkward positions. Alice averted her eyes from them.

The walking distance to her house was not far, but much of the street was impassable, and she had to climb through rubble to finally reach her destination. When she finally arrived, she found only a huge crater where her home had once existed, and she stood for some time, unbelieving, trying to convince herself that she was in the right place. The neighbors' homes were gone as well.

She found Mrs. Benchley, the mother of her best friend, standing at the curb, numb with shock. Alice had been instructed to run to her in the event of danger, but when the bombs began dropping, she was caught unaware. Everyone thought the bombing was over after having endured a solid night of bombardment the previous evening, and she had barely made it to the local shelter in time. Mrs. Benchley and her family weren't as lucky.

Alice approached her and asked after her friend. Mrs. Benchley could barely shake her head, and she pointed to the ruins that had once been her home.

"Under there," she said. "Janie is under there. She's dead, Alice."

Alice backed away in disbelief. She had lost other friends since the bombings began five months prior, but the fate of her closest friend stunned her like none other. She turned and ran to find her mother. The hospital was about half an hour away from her home by foot, but despite the carnage in the streets, she reached it in half that time.

The Coventry-Warwickshire Hospital entrance was hardly recognizable, and the entire structure was barely standing. A large red cross had been painted on its roof and served to provide an easy and inviting target to the German bombers.

As Alice observed the rescue crews, staff and patients scurrying in and out and around the building, she was reminded of an anthill she had seen in a vacant lot in her neighborhood. When one of her friends would pour water or toss a burning match into their midst, the ants would suddenly rush wildly about in a panic, in all directions, just as everyone was doing now.

A crater three meters deep and two meters wide had formed outside the hospital entrance, and a narrow wooden plank had been thrown across to allow passage in and out of the main door. Alice approached it, searching for someone recognizable among the staff that might know where her mother was working.

There was no longer room inside the building to treat any more patients, so the ambulances were simply removing the injured from their stretchers and lining them up in rows on the ground near the entrance before rushing off as fast as they arrived to collect more.

Searching desperately, Alice eventually spotted an orderly she knew from her previous visits with her mother at the hospital. He was loaded down with a pile of bloodied towels and was headed toward the entrance. She rushed up to him and tugged at his jacket.

"Perkins!" she yelled at him. "Where is my mother? Have you seen her? I need to speak to her desperately!"

At first, he only shook his head as he hurried to the entrance, but finally called back, "If I see her, I'll tell her you're here!" before making his way across the wooden plank.

Alice would like to have rushed inside to search for herself, but she knew that her mother would be extremely busy, if she found her, and would not approve. Better to stay where she was and wait until her mother was able to take a break.

It was a long, uncomfortable wait. Observing a young nurse hectically moving from patient to patient, Alice asked if she could help, but she was simply waved away.

"Excuse me, Miss," she heard a meek voice call out to her.

Looking about, she spotted an elderly lady who lay beneath a thin blanket, clutching a small, panting, shivering dog to her chest. A bloody bandage was wrapped about her head. Alice approached the lady and asked what she could do to help her.

"That's very kind of you, dear," the lady said, smiling at Alice sweetly. "There's really nothing you can do for me, but my little Beatrice here, she could very well do with a bit of water if you might be able to manage it."

Alice assured her she would find water and began looking about. She quickly located a cart loaded with dirty trays, metal pans and several pitchers, one of which contained a small amount of water, which she poured into one of the pans that was slightly less dirty than the others.

She returned to the lady who barely managed a whispered "Thank you," as Alice held the pan out for the dog, who vigorously lapped up the water.

"I hope to have a dog of my own someday," Alice told the lady. "My father is away, fighting the war, but he promised me before he left that when he returns, he'll get me one."

"I call her Beatrice," the lady said painfully, "after Beatrice Lilly, my favorite entertainer. I'm so very glad she's here with me now. Dogs can be a great comfort, you know. A great ... comfort."

The lady closed her eyes and did not move. The dog stopped drinking, looked into her face and whined softly. Alice knew what that meant, but she couldn't bring herself to move.

Someone knelt behind her and reached over her shoulder to feel the artery on the lady's neck.

"She's gone, dear," a woman's voice said. "She no longer

feels any pain."

"Mother!" Alice cried, recognizing the voice and turning to embrace her.

"I've been so very worried about you," her mother said as Alice held to her close. "I couldn't get away, but I knew you would be smart enough to get to safety."

"Our house is gone," Alice said, sobbing into her mother's shoulder. "Everything. Everybody. All gone. Where will we live? What will we do?"

"We'll get by," her mother assured her. "You mustn't worry. You must continue to be brave. I know you can."

Her mother squeezed her shoulders and kissed her forehead, then turned to the old lady and picked up the little dog. She handed it to Alice who held it to her cheek. Lifting the thin blanket, her mother covered the lady's face.

"I have to get back to work," her mother said, looking around at the many patients lying about. "We moved many patients to the basement, and Doctor Finlay has told me I'm needed down there, so I've got to go. You'll have to stay here until I can find time to look for someplace for us to stay. I'm sure Doctor Finlay will help us. Now, listen, there is an underground one block away in case the bombing begins again. Do you think you'll be alright here by yourself until I return?"

Alice nodded reluctantly. "If you must go," she said.

"My dear, dear, Alice," her mother said, hugging her again. "We'll be all right. I can't tell you what a comfort it is to have such a brave daughter. I love you so very much."

"I love you, too," Alice replied.

Her mother pulled a handkerchief from her pocket and wiped tears from her face, then did the same for Alice. Looking down at the little dog, she roughed his fur and smiled.

"You know," she said, "I've been treating a little boy in the emergency ward inside who is very scared and in a great deal of pain. I'll bet this little dog would cheer him tremendously and help take his mind off his troubles. Why don't you let me take it inside for a visit?"

"I didn't think pets were allowed to go into hospitals," Alice replied.

"Well," her mother said conspiratorially, "I think everyone will be too busy to notice. Shall I give it a try?"

Alice sniffed and handed the dog to her mother who accepted it and then kissed her daughter on the forehead again before rising to her feet. She touched Alice's cheek and then she was gone.

Alice watched as her mother, cradling the dog in her arms, waited for a man to pass who was using the platform to exit the hospital. When the plank was free, she cast another smile back at Alice and started to cross. She was barely halfway across when the unexploded bomb, which lay, unknown to anyone, beneath the mud at the bottom of the crater, suddenly detonated.

The power of the blast instantly threw Alice back against the wall of a building behind her with such force that she was knocked unconscious as glass, smoke and bricks flew all around her. The unexpected suddenness of the explosion did not give her time before she lost consciousness to fully comprehend the last image she saw of her mother as her body was hideously blown apart before her eyes.

When Alice regained consciousness the next day, she found herself lying in a hospital bed with Doctor Finlay leaning over her, shining a light into her eyes. She could tell he was speaking to her in a soft, reassuring voice, but the sound was muted as her hearing had been temporarily impaired. She had survived the explosion with only minor injuries, however, which quickly healed with the doting doctor's gentle care.

In time the memory of her mother's final moments came back to her in her sleep, sometimes vividly, and she would waken from her nightmare in a sweat, screaming and sobbing, but there was no one there to calm and comfort her.

This night, however, as she wakened, she found she was not alone. Banner lay at her side, and he licked her cheek. She hugged him close and buried her face in his soft, warm fur until she was finally able to fall asleep again, this time feeling peaceful and loved. The collie remained with her much longer than usual and didn't leave until very early in the morning.

CHAPTER EIGHT

At breakfast the next morning, Ridley delivered Alice a written message from Captain Bramwell, accompanied by a bundle of three books tied together with twine. Mrs. Thorndike pretended to show no interest in the items, and Alice did not intend to give her the satisfaction of sharing them with her, so she took her time finishing her breakfast before returning to her room.

Loosening the twine about the books, she glanced at the titles: *Peter Pan*, *The Enchanted Wood* and *A Traveller in Time*. Tossing them aside, she enthusiastically ripped open the Captain's note.

Dear Miss Piper,

I must once again extend to you my apology, this time for sending you away so abruptly. While I apologize for the fright my warning may have given you, I nevertheless strongly urge you to exercise extreme care, for I assure you, the threat remains very real.

Though I have chosen to live a solitary life these many years, I found myself eagerly looking forward to your visit and regret that I made such a mess of it.

Why don't you drop in this morning and allow me to demonstrate for you some of the clever tricks Banner has mastered? I know he will enjoy performing them for you as much as I will enjoy your company. Please understand, however, that due to damage inflicted upon my nervous system during the war, I am sometimes subject to unprovoked and uncontrollable changes of mood such as you have already witnessed.

If I should feel such an attack beginning to overtake me during your visit, I trust you will understand if I unexpectedly withdraw to my house and beg you in advance to forgive me once again.

I shall look forward to our next meeting.

Sincerely,
Joshua Bramwell

Alice needed no further persuasion and was soon well on her way down the path leading to the Captain's residence. She found him at the gazebo by the lake, sitting at the little table with Banner lying at his side. As soon as she came into view, the collie rushed toward her barking and wagging his tail. She imagined he was saying to her, "I am so glad to see you! I have so much to tell you!"

The gazebo had been thoroughly cleaned and cleared of weeds and shrubbery.

"I'm pleased you could join me this morning. Please take a seat," he said gesturing to the other chair. "Banner can hardly restrain himself, as you can see."

As soon as she was seated, Banner sat beside her and rested his head in her lap, looking into her face as she patted him.

"I don't think I ever thanked you properly for saving his life," the Captain continued. "Quite the contrary, in fact. But I must tell you that when I settled down and realised what I had witnessed, it occurred to me that you are a very special young lady to have risked your life to save him, and I wanted to know you better."

"How could anyone not have done what I did?" Alice asked. "I couldn't let him drown."

"There are those," he replied, "who may have done that very thing. Such people believe we owe nothing to animals. To them, dogs are unimportant. They fail to recognize their beauty. They fail to see that a dog has a soul. They are blind. It takes a sensitive, caring person such as yourself to perceive the blessing God gave to us when he gifted us with a dog. My life is worthless, but the dog sitting beside you now doesn't believe that."

The Captain rose to his feet with difficulty.

"Now," he said, "I promised a demonstration of some of Banner's tricks. Let's see if he'll oblige us, shall we?"

Banner recognized what the Captain was preparing to ask him to do, and he rushed before him, eager to demonstrate. Without waiting for a signal, he lowered himself onto his front elbows in a mock bow. Alice clapped her hands and giggled.

"Excellent!" the Captain commended as he withdrew a small piece of dried meat and tossed it to him. Banner caught the treat in midair and responded with a bark that indicated he was ready for another command. There followed a series of tricks, most of them performed in response to gestures made with the Captain's hand. After the collie had shown off his ability to lie down, crawl, roll over, wave and several other behaviours, the Captain handed Alice a handful of dried meat pieces, and Banner repeated his repertoire for her as she laughed delightedly.

"And now, ladies and gentlemen, boys and girls of all

ages," the Captain said, doing his best to imitate a circus ringmaster, "may I direct your attention to the center ring, where the one, the only, the incomparable Banner the Collie shall perform one last amazing routine, guaranteed to entertain and astound one and all! To assist Banner the Magnificent, I shall need a young volunteer from the audience. Now, let's see …"

He looked about as if searching the faces of a large audience gathered around him.

"Ah!" he said, finally setting his sights on Alice. "Now, young lady, please provide our Banner with a personal item. Let's see, your pretty blue scarf, perhaps?"

Alice removed her scarf and handed it to the Captain.

"Excellent! Excellent!" he said and Banner barked again. "I shall now ask you, young lady, to find a hiding place. Some place where you think the star of our circus will never find you. When you are gone and safely hidden, I shall allow Banner to examine this scarf and instruct him to lead me to your hiding place. Do you understand, my dear?"

Alice nodded enthusiastically.

"Now then," the Captain continued, "when I say 'go,' I shall begin counting to one hundred. After I have finished, Banner and I will be not far behind. Are you ready?"

Alice nodded again.

"Very well," he said, turning Banner to face the lake. "Banner will not watch, so he will not know in which direction you will be hiding. Here we go. One, two …"

Alice eagerly ran toward the path and paused a moment, deciding which direction to travel before settling on following the route back to the main house. She ran so energetically that she was out of breath by the time she reached the stables and decided that would be a good hiding place.

Once inside, she found it had apparently stood unused for many years. Dust, cobwebs and decay had been allowed to accumulate while bridles hung on the walls outside the stalls were dry and withered. A rat scurried along a splintered rafter. She considered hiding elsewhere, but a room in the back of the building partially revealed through a half-opened door captured her attention, and she was drawn toward it.

Alice pushed aside the door, which squeaked on its rusty hinges. A dim light, filtered through a small grime-encrusted window revealed a grubby, unkempt room scattered with rat feces, cobwebs, water stains, and mold, the result of a leaky roof. Several pieces of luggage were stacked in a corner, and a large trunk dominated the far wall. An unsecured padlock hung from its latch. Alice was intrigued and decided to investigate.

Grasping the latch, she attempted to open the trunk, but was met with resistance. Holding her breath, she gave a second pull and managed to lift the lid until it fell noisily back on its hinges, revealing an interior filled with small leather boxes and stacks of yellowed papers and envelopes addressed to Captain Joshua Bramwell in lady's handwriting.

She opted to examine the boxes first and selected one bound in black leather, ten by twenty centimeters in size. Opening the lid, she discovered a medal in the shape of a Maltese Cross suspended from a red ribbon. In the middle of the cross was the image of a lion guardant standing upon a crown. Alice had no idea what the medal represented, but she guessed it must have been awarded for some sort of military bravery. She opened a couple of other boxes and found each contained similar medals and ribbons.

Exploring further, she lifted a large stack of envelopes that had been secured with green ribbon. Stamped across the front of each was a triangle shape and the words "PASSED BY CENSOR," followed by a censor number. Alice knew it wasn't polite to read other people's private mail, and she held the stack of letters in her hand as she considered whether to snoop further. In the end her better judgment lost the debate, and she removed the top envelope from the stack and started to pull the letter from inside.

The sound of Banner's bark as he approached the room startled her, and she panicked as he came rushing in, vocalizing his joy as he ran back and forth, delighted that he had found her. Without replacing the envelope she had removed back into the stack, she hastily tossed the items in her hand back into the trunk and slammed down the lid. It crashed down with a loud thump at the exact moment the Captain entered the room.

"Aha! Success! Well done, Banner! Well done!" he exclaimed jubilantly from the doorway. His enthusiasm was cut short, and he became silent as he became aware of his surroundings. His one eye roamed the room, taking in the scene.

"I thought all of this had been destroyed," he said, referring to the luggage. "I instructed Ridley to ..." He fell silent again as he noticed that Alice was standing in front of the trunk, Banner at her side. The guilty look on her face told him what she had been up to.

He shambled toward her and moved her aside with his

hand. Staring at the latch a moment as if dreading to touch it, he then slowly grasped it and threw back the lid. He could clearly see that the stack of letters had been disturbed. Picking up the loose envelope, he looked fixedly at the handwriting as a flood of memories engulfed him.

Alice, at first fearful that he would be angry with her for snooping, at last relaxed a bit, though not completely for she knew he could fly into a rage without warning.

"All of this," he said quietly, "all of this from ages ago, I thought it was gone and forgotten, but here it sits buried beneath the dust and cobwebs, just as it has been buried beneath the dust and cobwebs of my memory."

The Captain laid aside the letter and picked up the box containing the medal Alice had first examined.

"Do you know what's inside?" he asked as he handed it to her.

Alice nodded.

"There is nothing inside," he told her.

She was about to disagree with him when he continued.

"*Nothing!*" he emphasized. "Only worthless pieces of metal and cloth, signifying nothing. Paltry pieces of rubbish whose purpose was to make me feel better about all the men I killed and replace the lives of all those who died while serving under my command."

He retrieved the box from Alice and tossed it back into the trunk and grabbed the loose envelope before slamming the trunk lid closed. He sat down upon the lid and held the envelope in his hand, staring at the floor as Banner moved to sit beside him.

Remembering that Alice was watching him with curiosity, he softened.

"When I was a young man, the whole world was mine," he said quietly. "I was born into a wealthy family in the greatest country in the world. I was young, attractive, and I was engaged to the most beautiful, loving young lady I could ever wish for. I could ask for nothing more. Then came the war, the war to end all wars. My younger brother, Edward, and I rushed to enlist, and before we had even seen our first German soldier, we were promoted, he to lieutenant and I to captain. We couldn't wait to see action. How glorious we thought it would be!"

He laughed and shook his head.

"Our first encounter with the enemy, the very first, was also our last. Under my command, my men were the first to be blasted with gas. It was early in the war, and we were unprepared for such a weapon, so none of us had any masks. It was bedlam. Then came the mortar attacks. My men, my boys, we all took direct hits, followed by more direct hits. Edward was one of the first killed, blown apart right before my eyes. I continued to fight, but my entire unit was killed, some in the trenches and some later in the hospital. I, however, was less fortunate than they. I lived. My skin was seared raw by the mustard gas, and the right side of my body was almost completely blown away, leaving me with only one eye, one leg, and one arm I could manage. I could barely even be recognized as anything human. Through the years, the doctors tried everything they could to make me presentable, but my body would have none of it. My pride wouldn't allow me to submit to a wheelchair, so I learned to use a crutch. I endured surgery after surgery, much of it more painful than anything I experienced in the trenches. Finally, I just gave up. So did the doctors. They sent me home to live out my life in the state you see me now."

"But," Alice managed to say, nearly moved to tears, "what about your fiancée? What happened to her?"

"My fiancée," he said, shaking his head. "Oh, she wrote me the most encouraging letters while I lay suffering in that hospital bed in France. She told me that whatever happened to me, nothing mattered. She would be there to greet me when I returned, and our love would see us through. Our love! It took me some time after I returned to allow her to see my face. I kept it covered, you see, so I wouldn't shock her. As the weeks passed, I could see that she was uncomfortable being near me, and I realised she would never be able to share my life. One day I simply removed the covering from my face. I will never forget the look in her eyes before she hung her head and simply walked away. Later she wrote me a very remorseful letter but admitted she could never give me the support I needed. She said she would have to share my pain from afar."

He crumpled the envelope in his hand and tossed it aside.

"My one good eye was so badly damaged, I couldn't even shed tears. I vowed I would never see that expression on anyone's face again. I moved into the cottage where I live now, and I completely cut myself off from the outside world. Ridley serves me, Missus Thorndike looks after my house and my business under my direction, and Doctor Finlay looks after my health during brief visits. My only true friend, the only one who keeps me going, who lifts my spirits and remains by my side, steadfast, caring and full of love, is my dog, my Banner. I could ask for no better comrade."

"May I have my scarf back?" Alice asked, seeing a portion of it hanging out of his jacket pocket.

"Of course," he replied, handing it to her.

"My mother gave it to me before she died," Alice said as she laid it across her shoulders, and then began stroking Banner's head. "You're very lucky."

The Captain looked at her.

"I mean," she quickly added, "to have Banner. He's helped me too since I've been here. I wish he had been beside me when my mother died. I was with her when the bomb went off that killed her, you know. I saw her die."

"Oh, Alice, you poor girl!" the Captain said with surprise. "I didn't know."

Alice shrugged. "This is the first time I ever said that out loud. You're the first one I've told."

The two of them sat in silence.

"It's Banner, you know," the Captain said. "His presence has made it easier for both of us to open up. You're the first person I've spoken to like this in many, many years. An 11 year-old child! Funny, isn't it?"

Alice nodded.

"There's something I must ask you," she said after hesitating. "About the thing in the forest, are you sure it's real? It's not your imagination?"

The Captain stood and began pacing.

"You've been talking to the others," he said. "Missus Thorndike and the others, haven't you? They told you I'm mad and I imagine things, didn't they?"

"Why don't you call a policeman?" she asked.

"The Constable, the villagers, think I'm a lunatic, too. Well, of course they would. The mental case who lives by himself is imagining things in the forest. But it isn't imaginary. Banner sees it moving out there, watching us. It isn't wildlife, either. It's real. I don't know what it is, but it's real. So, what am I to do? I can't go after it into the forest in my condition. I'm not crazy, but if I can't stop it soon I very well may be. If I'm still alive, that is."

"Listen," he said, getting close, "I'm going to instruct Missus Thorndike to give you the key to your room. I want you to lock yourself in at night. Lock your door tightly, do you hear?"

Banner moved between them and stood staring up at the Captain.

"Captain Bramwell," Alice stammered as she backed away. "You're frightening me. Please stop."

He stood breathing heavily as he stared at her, realizing he was about to experience one of his anxiety attacks. He began petting Banner frantically as he tried to rein in his hysteria.

"Yes. Yes," he finally said. "I'd better go lie down now, before I …"

He abruptly turned and left. Banner followed.

Left alone, Alice felt an eeriness creep over her. A cloud passed overhead, darkening the small amount of light shining through the window. She couldn't get out of the stable fast enough.

Once outside, she stopped and looked up at the dark cloud hanging overhead before her attention was directed toward the forest.

She had to do something to help Captain Bramwell. She decided she must enter the forest and prove to him that there was nothing there.

She would take Banner with her, just in case there was.

CHAPTER NINE

After breakfast the next morning, Alice reported to Mrs. Thorndike. She found her deeply engrossed in the contents of several ledgers spread out on her desk in the study.

"I'll be with Captain Bramwell this morning, ma'am," Alice reported.

Mrs. Thorndike did not look up from her work but asked, "Are you keeping your schoolwork current? Are you following the lesson plan that was included with your textbooks?"

"Yes, ma'am," Alice responded. It was partially true, though not entirely. She knew Mrs. Thorndike would not go to the trouble of checking her work.

When Mrs. Thorndike had no further response, she left her to her accounts.

Alice couldn't have picked a gloomier day to explore the forest, and she was glad she had chosen to wear trousers. As if anticipating her excursion, the day had begun cold, damp and dreary, and the clouds hung oppressively low in the heavens. Darker, more sinister clouds lurked on the horizon, promising to deliver rain by day's end. She should have waited for more agreeable climate, but she was determined to complete her objective without further delay. The longer she waited the stronger and more bizarre her imagination became.

Her knock on the Captain's door was met, not unexpectedly, by a cheerful bark from Banner on the other side.

"Yes?" she heard the Captain's voice ask.

"It's me, Alice," she announced. "May I come in for a moment, sir?"

There was a pause before he replied. "One moment."

Alice knew why he delayed allowing her to enter. He likely needed time to cover his face.

"The door is unlocked," he finally said.

When she opened the door, Banner met her enthusiastically. She stepped around him and passed through the entry hall and into the book-lined study, where the Captain was sitting in the large leather chair studying a book that rested upon a metal stand before him. At least, to Alice, he seemed to be studying the book, whose author she could make out on the book's spine, was Charles Darwin. The Captain set down his wire rimmed spectacles.

"Good morning," he greeted her warmly. "You're getting an early start on the day, I see."

"I wonder if I might borrow Banner for a while?" Alice asked. "I thought perhaps I might like to explore the grounds around the house a bit, and I expect he would make a splendid guide."

"I'm sure he would be delighted to escort you about," the Captain answered and then addressed the dog. "What say you, old boy?"

The collie sensed he was being offered a chance to get out of the cottage, and he rushed through the entry hall to the front door and barked impatiently for Alice to follow.

"Thank you, sir," Alice responded as she followed Banner.

When she opened the door, the dog rushed out, but she paused there as the Captain called out to her.

"Only, Alice ..."

She knew what he was going to say.

"You mustn't go into the forest. I don't know what danger lurks there. You must stay away."

Alice said nothing as she withdrew.

Leaving the cottage, she walked down the path away from the forest, toward the main grounds of the estate as Banner gingerly trotted beside her, occasionally looking up at her as though he was asking where they were going. She glanced back as she left the Colonel's cottage behind her and saw him watching her from a window. She forced a smile and waved goodbye. He responded with a single nod.

The apprehension that consumed Alice as she contemplated the undertaking ahead of her weighed more heavily now that it required her to disobey the Captain's specific warning. She could only justify her disobedience with the knowledge that it was motivated by her attempt to bring him peace.

Circling around the front of the main house with Banner at her side, she made her way to the edge of the forest from a route that could not be seen from the Captain's residence. Standing before a line of trees that marked the boundary of the forest, she peered into the darkness that lay before her. A low, ominous moaning sound created by a subtle wind passing through the trees floated out from within, as if it were a ghostly warning.

"I suppose the longer we stand here the harder it will be to go in there, don't you think?" Alice asked Banner. He looked apprehensively into the gloom and then raised his nose to sniff what lay ahead. His tail was tucked tightly between his legs, which offered her no consolation.

"Come along, then," she said to him and started toward the trees. Banner whined and took two steps backward before barking a warning.

"Banner!" she scolded him. "What's wrong with you? I thought you were a brave, strong dog. What are you frightened of?"

He looked into her face, whining again, with an expression that pleaded with her not to continue.

Perhaps the Captain had taught him to stay out of the forest, Alice thought. He was only obeying the Captain. Sure. That must be it.

"Very well, then," she said to him. "If you haven't the courage to go with me, I shall have to go it alone. Goodbye."

Seeing no established pathway, she entered the forest slowly, swallowing heavily as she pushed aside the shrubbery. When she was several steps within the interior, she paused for a moment to allow her eyes to adjust to the darkness. Behind her, Banner was still barking. He trotted in a nervous circle twice before stopping and deciding he had been left no choice but to follow. Alice breathed more easily as he crept through the bushes to stand beside her.

Surveying her surroundings, she found that the landscape looked identical in all directions, and the overcast sky offered no ray of light. She worried that she might eventually become lost if she travelled far, but she was confident that Banner's sense of direction was better than hers. Placing all her faith in him, she resolved that she would worry about it no further.

The trees rose so tall above her, she was unable to see their highest point, and the branches of each tree reached so wide, they intermingled with the neighboring branches, creating a thickness that seemed impenetrable. Stepping forward, the density of the shrubbery and trees required her to change directions several times to seek an opening through which she could pass. She found herself frequently stumbling over the roots of large trees that extended outward over the ground like the tentacles of a sea creature. Alice's determination wavered several times, and she considered giving up.

She was startled by a sudden movement in the brush before her as a rabbit darted by. Banner was eager to give chase, but she managed to restrain him. She encountered several more rabbits and a few squirrels as she ventured on, but their appearances were always brief as they scurried to safety.

After struggling for nearly half an hour with the many obstacles along the way, her efforts were rewarded with the discovery of a small clearing amid the trees. Pausing to catch her breath, she observed that the trees and vegetation beyond were less dense, offering her easier passage.

Banner acknowledged the open space at once by merrily rushing to greet it, accompanied by his persistent barking. His appearance startled a large flock of birds, previously unseen within the low-growing greenery that covered the floor of the opening. As they rose into the air, his excitement was further stirred, and he rushed after them into the woods.

Alice desperately called him to return, but her commands went unheeded as Banner receded into the forest. She heard his barks as they echoed amid the trees and then begin to fade as he was drawn further into the distance. She rushed to follow the sound before it vanished completely. She had not had time to catch her breath sufficiently before giving chase, and she felt her chest burning as she gasped for air. She halted momentarily to gather her strength.

As she stood, she became aware that Banner was no longer barking. She screamed his name several times before resuming her chase in the same direction she had last heard him, then paused and called out again. Her strength drained, she collapsed, leaning her back against a tree. With all the wind left to her she called out two more times.

"BANNER! BA …"

Before the name left her lips the second time, there was a rustling in the bushes, and Banner stepped out from their midst. He stood looking at her with his head slightly tilted, as if to ask, "What? Why are you shouting?"

"You naughty, naughty boy!" she gasped with a mixture of anger and joy.

Banner turned to leave again but then stopped and turned back to her as if expecting her to follow before running away in the direction from which he had just appeared. Alice moaned with exasperation and staggered to her feet to follow him.

She hadn't travelled far before she came upon a gurgling mountain stream. Banner was drinking from it noisily. He paused long enough to look up at her before he resumed his drink. Alice was barely able to carry herself to the water's edge, where she collapsed on her stomach and joined Banner in a cool, refreshing drink.

When her thirst had been quenched, the two of them sat beside each other, scrutinizing their surroundings. The low rumble of distant thunder rolled among the clouds.

Other than German bombs, she had never encountered personal danger, let alone sought it out, and she hadn't considered how she might deal with the source of the mystery she was seeking, should she encounter it.

"This was such a stupid thing to do!" Alice confided to Banner. "I could be lost already and what if you can't lead us out of here? We could both die before anyone would find us. Why didn't I use my brain?"

She slapped her forehead, and Banner gave her a quizzical look.

"Well," she said with a sigh, "I don't suppose there's any point sitting here feeling sorry for ourselves. Come along, boy."

Alice stood and found her way across the stream with a few carefully placed steps on a series of stones that jutted up out of the water. During her crossing, Banner came bounding by, splashing her along the way, and she screamed with displeasure. He reached the other side first and waited until she stepped onto dry land before shaking the water from his fur onto her. Alice upbraided him, and he responded with a wagging tail.

She wished she had brought a warmer jacket with her, but even more than that, she wished she had brought a towel. She vocalized a subdued growl before venturing on, with Banner in the lead, following the downward flow of the stream.

Several minutes had passed before Banner began to sniff the ground, pausing occasionally to analyze the smell of a plant they passed.

"What is it, boy?" Alice asked. "Have you picked up something?"

Banner was far too absorbed in the aromas he was encountering to acknowledge her, and as he moved along, he gradually began walking faster and sniffing more rapidly. Minutes later his nose led them to a narrow path that led from the side of the stream, through the shrubbery and into the forest.

Judging from the fact that the greenery along its route had been crushed underfoot by someone or some *thing*, but was not yet dead, Alice surmised that it was a fresh trail recently visited. It was too heavily trodden to have been created by a rabbit or even a wolf, she theorized. The thought of a wolf caused her to shudder. What if the Captain had been wrong about their presence? No, she decided, it must be deer. And yet, she had seen no deer.

Banner held his head low and slowly began following the path, glancing from side to side cautiously as he walked.

Alice picked up a solid stick that lay nearby, breaking away a few small branches to create a walking staff that she hoped might also serve as protection should she need it. She followed Banner, heeding his watchful wariness.

Minutes later, he stopped and lifted his head to sniff the air ahead. Satisfied that he had identified its source, he trotted forward. They hadn't gone far before they came upon another clearing, much smaller than the one discovered earlier. Stopping to survey the scene, they observed that the entire ground before them was inhabited by a large number of sizeable birds. They were scavengers, busy picking at something that was spread throughout the area as they fought among themselves for their share of whatever it was. They were not at all alarmed by the presence of interlopers.

Banner would not tolerate such insolence and rushed into their midst, barking ferociously. A few birds flew up but not away. Most simply scattered but remained on the ground, refusing to yield their treasure, and as soon as Banner had moved them from one spot, they would reassemble after he had passed.

Peering into the spaces Banner managed to clear, Alice could see that the birds were obsessed with the remains of three or four wild animals. Rabbits, presumably, judging from the size of the bones and the pieces of shredded fur, but she could tell that the birds were not what had killed them. The birds were dining on leftovers. Other animal fur and bones, stripped clean, were scattered about the area, indicating it was a place that had been used for some time to slaughter animals, though she knew not for how long. Nearby, she noticed a rabbit carcass dangling from the end of a wire that hung from a tree branch. Several birds clutched at the remains and picked at it as it swung under their weight and movement. She waved her staff at the birds, and they noisily dispersed, only to return again.

She wondered, had these animals been killed for their meat or simply for the satisfaction of killing? Alice had seen enough, and she called Banner to her side as she navigated the circumference of the area to pick up the trail where it resumed on the other side.

They followed the pathway another 15 minutes before it delivered them to another mysterious scene. They halted again as Alice tried to figure out what they had discovered.

A wide passage had been torn among the branches of the trees beginning from the very top and descending deep into the forest. It looked to Alice as if a giant monster had pushed its way through, angrily mangling everything in its way as it fell to the ground. She considered, for a moment, how little protection her staff and her dog would offer against such a creature. They continued to follow the path that wound toward the alley in the trees. The sky above them rumbled.

Along the way, Alice noticed several pieces of unrecognizable metal of all sizes strewn about the ground, and Banner paused briefly to sniff them. Had the giant ripped them from some man-made machine sent to do battle with it? Who would have won such a battle?

As they neared a point at which the damage came close to the ground, she noticed another path that led off from the one they were following. She called Banner to follow her as she sought to learn its destination and very soon came upon a heavily trampled area around four mounds of dirt. There was no mystery as to the reason for their existence. Alice knew they were graves. There were no markers, and they appeared to have been dug recently.

She backed away and called Banner to follow her as she returned to the main pathway. Pausing at the intersection between the two trails, she once again considered abandoning her quest, but now that she knew that whatever had taken place in the area had involved humans, not monsters, she was more curious than frightened. Well, she admitted to herself, a little less frightened. A human had survived long enough to bury those who hadn't survived, so she guessed that someone had wound up lost in that area and didn't know how to find a way out of the forest. She had to learn the survivor's fate. She pushed on.

Her question was answered soon afterward. There came a point where whatever had fallen from the sky must have hit the ground, tearing up the forest floor before skidding to a stop. Before her, she found the large object sitting at the end of the skid marks beneath piles of branches and shrubbery that had been placed over it in an attempt to conceal it from above.

Approaching the thing, her suspicion was soon confirmed as she identified it as a large aircraft. Advancing closer, she was able to see much of its body, as the camouflage was only concerned with concealing it from overhead, while the lower portion was left mostly visible from the ground. Its right wing had been severed as well as large portions of the double tailfins, all of which likely lay under brush nearby. Both of the twin propellers were bent or detached, and all of the glass that had covered the nose and stepped cockpit was broken. However, a tarpaulin had been thrown over the section the pilot must have occupied. The aircraft lay lopsided on its stomach since the landing gear had buckled beneath it. The fuselage, peppered with bullet holes, was long and narrow and about 16 meters in length, and Alice nearly screamed when she spotted the straight-arm bar cross painted on its side and a portion of a swastika image that remained on a damaged tailfin.

Holding her staff high, she wheeled about, looking for any survivors that might be lurking about, while Banner busied himself sniffing around the area. A seat had been removed from the interior of the plane and was placed beside a fire pit that was outlined with stones. A makeshift spit was placed across it, and two wooden logs that had been thrown in the center were glowing dimly. A plate, a cup and several eating utensils were placed at the edge of the pit, and a small mound of trash, consisting mainly of canned goods, was piled nearby. She shuddered at the thought of a German somewhere nearby.

Figuring she had enough information to confirm the Captain's suspicion that something bad was indeed lurking in the forest, she prepared to depart. Alice quietly called Banner. He was not around. Quickly searching the area, she continued to call his name before she spotted him. He was standing on his hind legs on a box that had been placed beneath an opening in the belly of the aircraft. A port door hung from hinges attached to the entryway, and Banner was resting his front legs inside the plane as he investigated what lay within.

"Banner! No!" Alice called out, but she was too late. At that moment he pulled himself up and into the interior of the plane.

As she rushed to the hole into which he had disappeared, she noticed an odd sound coming from within. Tossing her staff aside, she cautiously stepped onto the box and slowly lifted her head into the entryway. As soon as she had risen far enough for her eyes to clear the hole, she was startled by something that rushed directly at her. It was Banner, welcoming her aboard.

"Banner!" she angrily said to him. "What are you doing? Get out of there at once! We have to get away from here! It's dangerous!"

She stopped as she once again noticed the peculiar sound, which she then recognized was coming from the cockpit. Using her forearms, she pulled herself higher to afford a better view of the front of the plane and was finally positioned to see into the pilot's cabin. The sound, she discovered, emanated from a radio near the dashboard. A dim light illuminated the controls on its face, and amid its static transmission Alice could hear a male voice speaking in German. She started to retreat back down through the port.

Banner, who had moved to position his head next to hers as she lowered herself down, was looking over her shoulder to the ground below. He began to growl. Alice froze.

In a split second, she felt her ankles tightly grabbed from behind as she was simultaneously yanked downward, barely missing the box beneath the entryway as she hit the ground hard, landing on her back. Banner barked ferociously and was prepared to jump to the ground when the port door was slammed shut and latched, closing him in and muffling his frenzied barking.

CHAPTER TEN

Alice's head was swimming, her back ached, and her fall left her breathless, but before she could find energy to move, her ankles were again grasped and she was pulled from the underside of the aircraft. For a moment, as she lay motionless, she could only stare wide-eyed at the colorless sky above her, but as she regained her senses, a grey figure leaned over and into her field of vision.

He was about 38 years old, and a light growth of beard covered his thin face. His eyes were a fierce shade of blue like none Alice had ever seen before. His thin lips were held tight and straight and never yielded a smile. His eyebrows, perfectly shaped, were always raised high on his forehead, while his eyelids were half-open. There was a bruise on his left cheekbone. The combined effect accurately presented the image of an individual who was suspicious, skeptical, cold and dangerous.

"Tell your animal to stop that yapping before I stop it for him!" the man said in a thin voice, enunciating his words precisely, in English, with a slight German accent. He was pointing the barrel of a handgun close toward Alice's face.

"Banner! No! Lie down! No barking!" she called out, and he responded by reducing his bark to a low, constant growl.

"Better," the man said before stepping back, "Now, get to your feet."

Racked with pain, Alice, with some difficulty, made an attempt to stand. Before she had fully risen, the man impatiently grabbed her arm and pulled her up, then gave her an angry shove back. He stood before her, pistol in hand, dressed in military trousers and boots. His shirt, open at the collar, was soiled and ripped at one shoulder, which Alice figured he may have come by during the plane crash or while performing manual labor around his camp.

The man glanced at his wristwatch.

"Your name is Alice, I believe," he said, "and you are a guest at the monster-man's estate nearby. Am I correct?"

"How do you know that?" she asked.

"I know that because I am a trained professional," he answered as he settled himself in the seat by the fire pit. He pulled a cigarette from his pants pocket and made a show of lighting it with an expensive-looking lighter. "I am here in this predicament because of sheer bad luck. I should never have chosen to fly with the incompetent fools who crashed the plane."

"You've been stealing food from our kitchen," Alice declared.

"Sit down. You look dizzy," he said with a laugh, gesturing with his gun. "Or is that the way you always look?"

Banner had meanwhile moved to the front of the plane and was now barking through one of the broken windows. Alice ordered him to stop barking. He complied but continued to grumble as she lowered herself to the ground.

"Where did you learn to speak English?" she asked the German.

"Oh, I am a very intelligent man. In fact, I speak several languages fluently. If I seem immodest it is only because it happens to be true. I have earned a great deal of respect and I am a very important person in my homeland."

"If you're so important, what were you doing on this

airplane? You were bombing Coventry, weren't you?"

"Indeed. Quite successfully, in fact. Quite successfully. We would have made it back to our base across the channel had it not been for an annoying little Spitfire. A rather noisy and furious electric storm prevented anyone from noticing us when we crash landed. Nevertheless, I assure you the crew died a valiant death, knowing that they destroyed so much of …"

He stopped, making a sudden realization, and assumed an expression of mock concern.

"Oh, dear," he said, pretending to be surprised. "You are from Coventry, are you not? Perhaps your relatives, your playmates, may have been injured or killed in the bombing, yes?"

Alice crossed her arms and pouted.

"Tsk-tsk. Such a pity," he said. "So unnecessary. If only your foolish British leaders would surrender to us, all of this could be avoided. Our Fuehrer will win this war eventually. Resistance is so very stupid."

"My father is a British soldier. He's away right now, killing Germans like you."

"Not like me, you stupid little thing. Not like me. I am not like the others, and your poor father will soon die like all of his compatriots. Such a pity. However, I will not waste my time discussing the war with someone of your immature intelligence."

"They'll find you here very soon, you know. They'll capture you and put you in a prison camp or something far worse."

The man smiled and tossed his cigarette into the fire pit.

"I'm sorry to disappoint you, my dear, but that will not happen. I will not be here much longer."

He made a slight bow toward her.

"I have not introduced myself. I am Major Richter, and I am a very important, very valuable asset to my country. I won't tell you why, of course, but you can be certain I am telling you the truth. My leaders know exactly where I am, and I will be rescued very soon. They cannot afford to let me perish here."

He pulled a small, worn notepad from his pants pocket and held it up for her to see.

"I was able to gather some very important information from this mission," he said and then returned it to his pocket. "That information will greatly assist me with an important project I'm developing. So, you see, all of the people who were killed in the bombing did not die needlessly."

"What are you going to do about me?"

The Major smiled and stood. He holstered his pistol with his right hand as he reached behind his back with his left, withdrawing a dagger that had been sheathed on his belt. Holding it before him, he rotated it in his hand, displaying it for Alice's benefit.

"Rather pretty, don't you think?" he asked. "I always wear it on my belt beneath my jacket. It isn't military issue, of course, but I have carried this with me at all times, ever since I was a young boy about your age. My father gave it to me on my birthday before he died in the last war, and I practiced throwing it day and night until I became quite accomplished at it. Shall I demonstrate?"

Alice did not respond, and he began looking about the

area for a target. His eyes landed on Banner, who was watching him intently from the broken window.

"Ah!" the Major exclaimed as he pulled his arm back, taking aim at the collie.

"No!" Alice screamed over Banner's renewed barking.

She rushed toward the major in an attempt to seize the dagger, but he easily grasped her wrist with his free hand.

"You are very devoted to that creature, I see," he hissed at her as he gripped her wrist tightly, "and he to you, no doubt."

"Let me go!" she growled as she tried to wrestle her arm free.

When he made no effort to release her, she kicked one of his shins. He reacted by angrily pushing her to the ground and followed by forcibly throwing his dagger at her. Its point struck firmly in the ground only an inch from her neck. Startled, she stared wide-eyed at the blade, realizing the Major was watching and eagerly waiting for her to make a move to grab it.

Finally, assured she wasn't going to play his game, he stepped forward and reclaimed his dagger before turning toward Banner, who was barking wildly.

"Shut up, you filthy beast," the Major shouted, but Banner was not about to comply.

"No, Banner! No!" Alice yelled to him as she got to her feet. "No barking! Sit!"

Obeying temporarily, Banner drew back.

"My parents gave me a little doggie as a gift when I was a young boy," the Major reminisced, "He didn't live long."

Turning back to Alice, he asked, "Now where were we?"

"You killed all those animals I passed along the trail, didn't you?" she asked. "With that knife?"

"I was simply amusing myself," he said with a shrug. "Oh, I butchered and ate some of them, but I did it mostly just to keep in practice. Such a lot of animals there are in this forest, have you noticed?"

"But you didn't just kill them, did you? Some of them were tortured."

"They are only animals," he scoffed, waving her off with the blade of his dagger. "Like your doggie over there. Only animals. Unimportant animals."

He said the last two words with a deliberateness that chilled Alice.

"So," he continued as he paced slowly about, "what to do about you, I wonder. Now that you have found me, how can I stop you from telling the others?"

He stopped and withdrew his pistol, pointing it in her direction.

"I could simply put a bullet in your head, of course, but that might be heard by someone nearby, your crippled monster-man perhaps."

"Don't call him that," Alice said angrily.

"No," he continued, "shooting you would be foolish, wouldn't it? On the other hand ..."

He holstered his pistol and concentrated on his dagger.

"On the other hand," he considered, "I could easily slit your throat, couldn't I, you and your doggie? I could toss your bodies with the other dead animals in the small clearing along the trail. The birds there are excellent scavengers. There wouldn't be much left when they finish with you. Yes, that's a very good idea, only ..."

He paused to relish the terrified look on Alice's face.

"Only," he resumed, "it wouldn't take long before you were missed, and soon those idiots in the village nearby would come searching for you, and I'm not ready to leave just yet. Very soon, but not just yet. Hmmm. What do you think, little girl? What would you do if you were me?"

"If you let me go," she replied, "Banner and me, I promise I won't say a word until after you've gone. I promise."

"Ah! But how do I know I can trust you? You are a little girl, and my country is very anxious for my return. It's very important to them. If you forget your promise to me, well, it might not turn out so well, mightn't it? Unless ..."

It was apparent to Alice that he had already devised a plan to deal with her. He drew close.

"Perhaps you already know," he said in a near whisper as he held the dagger close to her face, "I have been watching you and everyone at the estate for some time now, through my binoculars, watching from a distance while hidden here in the forest. Your doggie there knows, and your monster-man apparently knows as well. You don't even know that in the darkness of night, when your doggie leaves your room and returns to the monster-man, I sneak into the house and help myself to some of the food and cigarettes. Do you know, I even creep up to your room at night and watch you sleeping? Did you know that, little girl?

Alice's heart pounded loudly, and she shook her head.

"So, you see, if I should let you go and if you should be foolish enough to tell anyone, *anyone*, of my existence here, well … I will know and it would not turn out well for you, or your monster-man or all the rest. Even your doggie. Especially him. He would be the first to go. One carefully aimed bullet in his skull. I would still have plenty of bullets for the others. Wouldn't they be surprised?"

"How can you be so evil? You enjoy being that way, don't you?"

"What I do must be done," he said, angrily grabbing her arm. "Why shouldn't I derive some pleasure from it?"

Alice managed to pry his hand from her arm.

"You're a very sad man. You would never understand. Even my dog over there is far more human than you'll ever be!"

The Major clenched his jaw and consulted his watch again as a few scattered raindrops began falling.

"I have no time to debate psychology with you," he replied and then yanked away the scarf tied loosely around her neck.

Alice struggled with him to retrieve the scarf, but he brandished the dagger in her face, and she stepped back. He tossed the scarf back to her.

"Put this around the dog's neck and prepare to leave," he ordered. "Hurry."

Alice unlatched the entryway and was eagerly greeted by Banner, who licked her cheek. She tied her scarf around his neck.

"Need I remind you to keep that animal under control?"

126

the Major asked, as he aimed the point of his dagger toward the collie.

Alice held tight to Banner's makeshift collar as he jumped from the box under the aircraft to the ground, pulling and barking at the Major.

"Now it is going to rain very soon," he said, "quite heavily I'm sure, so you'd better hurry."

As Alice passed the Major, Banner growled and tugged at his improvised collar, attempting to engage him. The Major stepped back slightly out of reach and waved the dagger in his face.

"Don't tease him! Stop it!" Alice shouted as the collie grew angrier.

Laughing cruelly, he taunted Banner further by waving the dagger in Alice's face and pretended to stab her. As the Major waved the weapon about, his sleeve pulled back enough to expose the thin, pale skin of his wrist. Banner focused on that white wrist. It was an irresistible target.

"Stop it! I can't control him when you do that!" Alice admonished as she backed away, pulling at the dog with all her strength.

The Major pointed to a path he had created that led into the woods.

"Very well, then. Follow that path there," he told her. "It leads directly back to the estate. If you had taken that route through the forest when you came, you would have found me much sooner with far less trouble. Go now, quickly."

Alice needed no second invitation. She dragged Banner by her side as she made for the pathway.

"Don't forget," the Major called after her, "I will be watching you. The life of that animal at your side is in your hands!"

The Major watched Alice depart as the rain began falling heavily. When she was out of sight he turned and entered the aircraft. Making his way to the cockpit, he seized the microphone and responded to the radio voice that was calling for him.

As he waited for an incoming message, he cursed himself again for joining the bombing mission that had placed him in such a vulnerable position. He needed to study firsthand details of the bombshells as they rained down upon the cities. The German military were very stingy with their weapons and had refused his request for a drop on simulated targets at home, leaving him no option but to accompany a mission performing the real thing. He was certain the information he gathered would prove invaluable in the design of the weapon he was secretly developing. He was equally certain that when it was completed, it would be of such power it would mean the end of the war. No other country would have a power equal to it. He had been careful to keep much of the design plans secret from even his own government, which was why he was now confident he would be rescued.

The radio message he received brought a wide smile to his lips. He was to be rescued soon. He worried, though, that the girl might not be able to keep his secret long enough for that to happen. She did seem to be insolent and defiant.

He figured he would have to kill her anyway.

CHAPTER ELEVEN

By the time Alice returned to the estate, she had been drenched by a heavy rain. She apologized profusely for Banner's wet condition when she returned him to the Captain and explained she had been "down the road" and lost track of time before being caught in the downpour. She quickly excused herself and ran back toward the main house, not allowing the Captain time to ask any uncomfortable questions.

Avoiding the household staff, she stealthily made her way upstairs to change into dry clothing. Shedding her wet things, she knew Anna had given up complaining to Mrs. Thorndike about finding her garments in slovenly condition each day. Since she befriended Captain Bramwell, it appeared to the maid that Alice had been given his permission to dress in whatever unkempt condition she wished and was exempt from the rules the head housekeeper would otherwise enforce. In any event, Alice knew she was facing a threat far greater than provoking Mrs. Thorndike's ire. As she changed, she wondered if her body was shivering due to the cold rain or the danger she had encountered.

Later that afternoon, Alice approached Mrs. Thorndike in the study.

"Excuse me, ma'am," she said. "Captain Bramwell said he left instructions for you to give me a key to my room. Might I have it now?"

Mrs. Thorndike made a show of removing her glasses, setting them on the desk in front of her, folding her hands and casting Alice her customary scowl of disapproval.

"You and Captain Bramwell have become solid

comrades, haven't you?" she asked. "All of these long years he's been secluded in that cottage, no outside contact with anyone. Now you appear and suddenly he's become an affable, congenial uncle. I suppose it's another phase of that sad, tragic condition of his that it's come to this. His only friends are a dog and an 11-year-old girl."

Mrs. Thorndike shook her head in disbelief. Alice chose not to confront her. She knew any quarrel would be in vain.

"May I have the key, please?" she asked.

The head housekeeper slowly opened the center drawer in front of her and withdrew an envelope, tossing it on the desk.

"Is he still trying to scare you with that nonsense about a phantom in the forest?" she inquired. "Do you really think some evil spirit will come for you in the night? You may be a prodigy, but only an immature child would believe such nonsense."

Alice felt she would burst, but with great effort, she managed to restrain herself from blurting out her great secret. Instead, she collected the envelope from the desk and started to leave. At the door she couldn't resist one comment.

"One day you'll regret you said that to me," she said. "You'd better lock your door tonight as well, Missus Thorndike."

Alice turned and left as Mrs. Thorndike laughed sarcastically.

That night, when Banner visited her, she cuddled him closely. Sensing her fear, he remained awake the entire time he lay next to her, and when the Captain whistled for him to return, he had to do so repeatedly. The collie was very reluctant to leave the girl, but finally acquiesced, slowly walking to the door. Alice noticed his absence and awoke to find him in the doorway, looking back at her with concern and whining.

"It's all right, Banner," she said as she stepped out of bed and knelt to comfort him. "You look out for the Captain. I promise I'll be all right until morning. We'll figure a way out of this. Together. You'll see."

She gave him a slight nudge, and he warily walked away. When he'd gone, she went to her window to make sure he made it safely to the Captain. When she was assured of that, she closed her door and carefully locked it, then rushed back to bed.

Throughout the night she thought she could hear sounds downstairs and in the hallway outside her door. She couldn't determine if it were her imagination. She feared that it might not be.

She wrestled with ideas to defeat the demon if she should encounter him again. As she played out each scenario in her head, they all ended badly.

The next morning being a Sunday, Alice tried her best to be excused from services under the pretense of an upset stomach. She wanted to stay near Banner and watch after his safety. Mrs. Thorndike would have none of it.

"Nonsense!" she exclaimed. "Get dressed and be quick about it."

During the service, Alice stared at the floor and avoided all eye contact. When the last prayer had been spoken, she pushed ahead of the others and rushed past the vicar as she headed straight for the car, hoping she wouldn't have to socialize. Her behaviour didn't escape Mrs. Thorndike's notice as she attempted to evade Phipps and Mayor Applebee, who made their usual effort to engage her in conversation.

Mrs. Richardson took advantage of Mrs. Thorndike's delay by rushing to Alice and attempting to hand her a small envelope.

"Alice, dear," she said to her. "Please pass this note to Captain Bramwell. I'm requesting him to allow you to join the children later this afternoon at the schoolhouse. We're going to plant a victory garden, and we would very much like you to join us."

Alice made no attempt to accept the note.

"I have to get back to the estate," she said, looking straight ahead. "It's extremely important. I won't be able to attend. Thank you. Good day."

"Oh, I'm sorry," Mrs. Richardson responded. "I would so love to earn your friendship."

"You heard what she said," Mrs. Thorndike interrupted from behind. "Good day."

Mrs. Richardson stood aside, and Mrs. Thorndike, Anna and Mrs. Belmore took their seats. Ridley promptly started the engine and guided the car down the road.

When they arrived home, Alice hurried to her room and hastily changed out of her church dress into casual wear. Ridley had just parked the car in the garage and was hanging the keys on a rack on the wall as Alice passed on her way to the Captain's cottage.

"Excuse me, Miss," he called to her. "I couldn't help but notice. You seem greatly disturbed. Are you well?"

"Quite well, thank you, Ridley" she responded, continuing on her way.

Ridley watched her as she walked on. He was not convinced and thought it might be best to broach the subject with the Captain later.

Nearing the Captain's cottage, Alice could hear his voice calling for Banner to return to him.

She knew it! Banner would make every attempt to finish with the devil in the forest. Her heart was beating wildly as she ran to the rear of the cottage. She found the Captain looking toward the woods as he shouted to his dog, who was making for the woods.

"Banner! Come back here! Now!" Alice screamed angrily.

The collie stopped and looked back at her, and she ran to him. As she approached, he hung his head and tail. He knew he had done wrong.

Alice reached him and clutched the fur around his neck in both hands.

"You cannot go back there! Not ever!" she reprimanded him, looking into his face but speaking low enough to prevent being overheard by the Captain.

Seeing the sad look in his eyes, she couldn't resist following her reprimand with a tight hug around the neck. Standing, she told the collie to come with her, and she kept one hand on his back as they walked back to the Captain.

"Since yesterday, it's all I can manage to keep him away from that damned forest," the Captain lamented as they joined him. "He's always resisted the urge to go exploring there, but now it seems to have become an obsession."

Banner picked up his ball and invited Alice to toss it for him. She obliged by throwing it toward her left, and he anxiously raced after.

"Perhaps," Alice said, "you should watch him very closely and keep him locked in after dark."

While they watched, Banner retrieved his ball but paused before running back to them. He dropped his toy and looked toward the forest. Alice nervously called him, and he finally reclaimed his ball and returned, dropping it at her feet. She picked it up and handed it to the Captain.

"In fact," she stated, "I don't think he should come to my room at night. At least, until he outgrows this obsession."

The Captain reacted with surprise.

"Well," she hastily added, "you told me to keep my room locked, remember? If I do that, he won't be able to return to you at night and what if he wanders off to the forest while I'm sleeping?"

"Then perhaps he should stay with you at night," the Captain offered, "behind your locked door."

"No," she said, shaking her head. "He should stay with you. I'll be all right, I promise."

"How can you be certain of that?" The Captain was becoming suspicious.

"It's just … It's just a feeling I have."

Banner barked to resume his game of fetch, and the Captain tossed the ball a short distance away.

"Then you sense it, too," the Captain said, looking wide-eyed into the forest. "It's grows nearer, closing in on us."

Alice struggled to caution him without revealing her

secret.

"Well, whether something really exists or not, it won't do any harm to be careful, will it?"

He nodded.

"You know it's real, too. I can see it in your face," he said to her.

Alice didn't realize her face was so easy to read. She quickly turned away and made a feeble attempt to avoid his scrutiny by calling Banner to rejoin them.

"I'd best return to the house for luncheon. If you don't mind, I'll drop in to see Banner again before supper."

The Captain nodded his approval, and Alice knelt to pet Banner before turning to leave. He watched her go and then cast an apprehensive look toward the forest. Calling Banner to follow him, he retreated to his cottage.

Inside, he entered his small bedroom and opened the top drawer of his dresser cabinet. Pushing aside several handkerchiefs, he located his old service revolver. After assuring himself that it was fully loaded, he shoved it into the side pocket of his jacket. Turning to leave the room, he was met by Banner, who sat in the doorway watching him curiously.

"I'm not even certain it will still fire after all these years," he said to the dog apologetically. "Whether or not it does, we'll be ready for whatever comes for us, won't we, you and I?"

CHAPTER TWELVE

Later that afternoon, as Alice was napping, there was an unexpected knock on her bedroom door

"Missus Thorndike says you are to come downstairs at once," Anna said breathlessly.

"What's happened?" Alice asked.

"The Captain has sent for you. You are to report to him posthaste. He says it's urgent," she replied.

Alice couldn't have put her books away any more rapidly, and in no time at all, she presented herself at the Captain's cottage. She found him in back at the edge of the forest, agitatedly pacing back and forth as he called desperately for Banner. He was carelessly attempting to walk fast and relied even more heavily on his crutch than usual. Alice was afraid he would fall and injure himself.

"Has he been with you?" The Captain asked wildly. "He hasn't, has he? No, of course he hasn't. How could I have been so careless?"

"Captain Bramwell," Alice said to him, her voice shaking, "You must be careful. It isn't safe for you to …"

"He was only out of my sight for a brief moment. I opened the door to allow him outside to relieve himself just a while ago, only he didn't come back to me. I kept calling him, *demanding* him to return to me, but he's nowhere to be found. I know we were being watched. I'm sure I saw someone out there. It was a man, I'm certain, watching us through field glasses."

Alice had to restrain herself from running about frantically as well, knowing Banner's life was in danger, but she knew she must not reveal to the Captain what true danger his dog was facing. Instead, she knew she must calm him and spare him from danger himself. She placed her hand on his right arm and walked him to the table and chairs on the turf.

"If he's gone into the forest, all we can do is wait and hope," she told him. "I'm sure he can take care of himself, and he'll be back very soon."

"If only I knew what he was up against," the Captain said worriedly as he looked over his shoulder. "Who knows what's out there?"

Helping him into a chair, she was overwhelmed with worry, and she tried desperately to think of a way to rescue Banner. The Captain noticed her nervousness and patted her hand.

"Yes, you're probably right," he reassured her. "He'll come leaping home soon."

Even with his face covered, Alice could tell he didn't believe it.

They remained at the table for nearly an hour, nervously watching for Banner's return. Ridley eventually appeared and offered them tea and sandwiches. Both declined.

Soon after Ridley cleared the table, he returned.

"Excuse me, sir," he addressed the Captain. "There's a gentleman here to see you, a Mister Phipps. He says he's the Local Defence Volunteer for the village, and he says it's quite important that he speak with you. Shall I send him away, sir?"

"Yes," the Captain growled. "Send him away."

"Very good, sir," Ridley replied and turned to leave.

"Bothersome idiots from the village," the Captain mumbled into his teacup. "Always wanting to talk to me about something insignificant, trying to satisfy their morbid curiosity. Local Defence Volunteer indeed!"

Suddenly he slammed his cup down on the table and called out for Ridley.

"Wait a moment! Ridley, come back!"

Ridley obliged, and the Captain stood and grabbed his sleeve.

"I've changed my mind. I wish to speak to him. Bring him to me at once!"

"At once, sir. Very good, sir," Ridley responded and hastily withdrew.

"Perfect timing!" he said to Alice, talking excitedly. "Just what we need right now."

Alice was apprehensive.

"Are you sure? I met that man in the village. He seems a bit full of himself. Not very competent, if you ask me."

"That doesn't matter," the Captain said, brushing her off. "He'll serve our purpose."

"Mister Phipps, sir," Ridley announced as he escorted him to the table.

Phipps, proudly dressed in his crisp, L.D.V. khaki uniform, stood at attention behind Ridley.

"*Sergeant* Phipps, if you please," he whispered to the butler as he passed him to leave.

Phipps took two soldierly steps forward, halted in front of the Captain, stamped his right foot briskly and delivered a snappy salute.

"Sergeant Phipps of the L.D.V., honored to be at your service, *sir*," he announced. When he saw that the Captain's head was wrapped in a scarf, he was, for a brief instant, thrown off guard, but immediately reassumed his respectful comportment.

"At ease," the Captain said with a slight nod, unimpressed with the display of military protocol.

" 'Course, that's an L.D.V. rank, not a military rank," Phipps said, relaxing a bit. "Nevertheless, I fully recognize you as my superior officer and will obey your command with respect. And might I add, sir, what an honor it is to be in the presence of an awardee of the Victoria Cross. Your valour in the face of …"

Alice suddenly understood what she must have found in the Captain's trunk in the stable. She didn't know exactly what the Victoria Cross represented, but she gathered enough to understand that it was an award presented for great bravery.

"Yes, yes, thank you, Phipps," the Captain interrupted him, waving aside his words of praise. "First things first. What did you wish to see me about?"

"I thought it best, sir," Phipps said very seriously, "to make you aware of my recently appointed responsibilities in the village, knowing your military standing and all."

"My former military standing," the Captain corrected him. "I am retired."

"Of course. Nevertheless, I would be very grateful if you would permit me to rely on your advice in matters pertaining to the war effort as well as your expertise relating to security and so on and so forth."

Phipps was prepared to deliver a lengthy patriotic speech he had prepared for the occasion, but the Captain cut him short.

"Yes, yes, most certainly. First, however, I wonder if I might ask a favor of you?"

"A favor of *me*?" Phipps stammered and then snapped back to attention. "I am at your service. Sir!"

"Recently I have become aware of something … *someone* I believe who may be watching, or perhaps spying on us from out there in the forest. I cannot be certain that it has anything at all to do with the war, but I don't think we should take any chances, do you?"

Phipps snorted.

"Cor blimey! I rather think not, sir. You leave it to me. I'll investigate this m'self, on the double."

He started toward the forest but was stopped by the Captain.

"Something you should know before you go, Phipps. My collie dog went searching the forest a while ago and hasn't returned. I can't help thinking he may be on to something, but I'd be beyond myself with grief if anything untoward has happened to him. Do look out for him for me, won't you? And if you should come across him, please bring him back safely."

Phipps became quite earnest.

"You may rely on me, sir. I'll see the noble animal home safe and sound, and be there a nutter or a Jerry out there, I'll bring him to heel as well."

Phipps saluted the Captain, who once again waved him off.

"Sir!" Alice called after Phipps as he headed toward the

forest. "I couldn't help but notice a small pathway to your left. Perhaps that will help you along."

"Splendid!" Phipps replied. "Thank you, lass!"

The Captain looked at Alice with suspicion, but she avoided his gaze.

"Won't you be needing a weapon of some sort?" Alice asked, "in case you should encounter a villain along your way?"

"Hmm," Phipps mused. "That hadn't occurred to me. The only weapon I own is me old Mk III rifle I brought home from the war. I'm not sure if it even still works. I'd have to go home and fetch it."

Suddenly his face lit up.

"I did acquire an old 18 pounder MK1 the army was about to scrap. We set it up in the village square as a sort of war memorial. I only have enough shells to fire a couple of shots, but I'm not too sure …"

"You'll have no use for a cannon on this mission, Phipps," the Captain interrupted.

"Here," he said, withdrawing his pistol from his coat pocket and handing it to him. "You can give it back to me when you return."

Phipps accepted the weapon as if he were being handed the crown jewels. Without further word, he again saluted and marched to the edge of the forest. Halting there, he remembered the pathway Alice had suggested, and redirected himself to follow that route. Soon he receded from view.

"He'll be all right," the Captain assured Alice, noting the concern on her face. "He survived a world war and came home in better condition than I, so that should give us some assurance."

Alice managed a smile, and together they sat at the table and waited. While they marked time, dozens of worrisome thoughts crowded her mind. She had heard no gunshots since Banner had been missing, but she couldn't rule out Richter's skill with a knife. She could only hope that Banner's sense of smell would warn him before his enemy could come close enough to do any harm. Still, it was unlikely the German would have passed up any opportunity to eliminate him, so warped was his love of killing. As for Phipps, his life was only in danger if he discovered the downed plane and its working radio. That remained a strong possibility as the trail he was following would take him directly there. In any case, she thought it best not to say anything to the Captain yet about her encounter with Richter unless there was some new development. If Phipps by chance found nothing, she could be risking the Captain's life by telling him what she was forbidden to reveal.

After a while, Alice clasped her hands and began silently praying.

"Would you like me to fetch the vicar?" the Captain asked.

"The vicar can't help us," she said with a shake of her head. "Only God can."

"You'll forgive me," the Captain said, leaning in to her, "I am beginning to sense you know what's actually out there."

"Well," she replied, searching for words, "whatever it is, it isn't a good thing, is it?"

The Captain decided not to pursue the conversation. How could this little girl know what was out there unless she had seen more than he, and if she did know more, why would she keep it secret? Nonetheless, his suspicions remained.

The afternoon passed slowly, but the two lookouts remained steadfast, save a quick visit to the privy for Alice. The Captain frequently stood and forced himself to pace about as best he could.

It was near dusk before they heard Banner's bark, echoing through the trees in the distance. Alice's heart raced as she rushed to greet him when he came leaping out of the darkness of the woods. He appeared unharmed, and he was full of energy as he licked her face before rushing to the Captain.

As he neared his master, Banner reined in his liveliness. The collie had learned through the years that a modified behaviour was necessary when approaching the Captain due to his fragile condition. If his injuries had not prevented him from doing so, the man would have shed tears as he carefully stroked his dog's head.

"Captain Bramwell!" Alice said, suddenly remembering. "Where is Mister Phipps?"

The Captain's joy suddenly diminished, and worry returned, but only monetarily, thanks to a hail from the forest.

"HALLOOO!" Phipps' voice called out from the trees, and in less than a minute, he had returned.

"Thank God!" the Captain exclaimed. "We've been on edge every second you were gone."

"Ahh," Phipps said, putting on a brave front. "I can look

out for m'self, though I must admit your collie dog there was a big help to me. I ran into him on the trail. He was headin' back home it appeared to me, but I'll be gobsmacked if he didn't turn around and lead me straight to a bleedin' bomber!"

"A German bomber?" the Captain asked with amazement.

"Right you are, sir. Looks like our boys must've made short work of 'im, though. All full o' bullet holes and such."

"Any sign of survivors?" the Captain inquired, pouring him a glass of water from a pitcher Ridley had left on the table.

"Ah, thank you, sir," Phipps acknowledged, as he reached for the glass. He took a couple of drinks before answering.

"Likely one or two, I suspect, judging from the camouflage piled on top. That, and the footprints in the mud around the plane. One set o' prints was most peculiar. Looks like someone rather small. A young woman, if you ask me, maybe some of the youths from the village snoopin' about. Only … if that were the case, I don't know why they wouldn't have reported their finding to me or the Constable. Most peculiar, that.

"Well, anyway, appears to me somebody must've survived the crash, buried the casualties, hung about for a bit and moved on."

"Moved on?" Alice asked anxiously.

"Right," Phipps confirmed. "See, it looks like whoever survived, destroyed the radio inside the cockpit. The way it was all torn apart and all, that didn't happen during the crash.

Well, Captain, you'd agree if you'd seen it yourself."

"But I was certain I saw someone out there this morning, watching from the woods," the Captain declared.

"Likely moved on since then."

"Perhaps."

"Speakin' o' which, I'd best trot on m'self. I'll call this in to the Home Guard unit commander over in Steffingshire. If he responds to my calls like he usually does, he won't make it round to the village for several days. Lot on his plate, I 'spect. Nevertheless, I'll get the word out. I'll report back to you tomorrow if I may, sir, just to make sure all's well at this end."

"Please do. Thank you for your time."

Phipps finished his glass of water and then reached into the pocket of his jacket.

"Oh," he said as he withdrew the Captain's pistol and handed it to him. "I'd best return this to you. Who knows if you might need it again someday?"

"It would probably do me little good. My eyesight ... my aim ... It's not what it once was."

Phipps looked at the Captain's one poor eye and understood his dilemma. He wanted to express sympathy, but he had sense enough to know it would not be well-received. Instead, he suddenly snapped to attention, delivered one final, respectful salute, which, as usual, was not returned, then turned on his heel and marched away.

The Captain collapsed into a chair and set the weapon on the table before him.

"Sit down, Alice," he said quietly.

146

She slowly obliged and Banner, still panting heavily from his exhausting excursion in the woods, laid himself at her feet. She was certain the Captain knew she had gone into the forest against his wishes.

"I'm sorry, sir," she said as she began to cry. "I know I disobeyed you, but I thought that if I could find out if anything was in the forest I could put your mind at ease. The German major caught me and threatened to kill Banner and everyone here if I told anyone about him."

"A German major?" the Captain asked with astonishment.

Alice nodded, wiping back the tears streaming down her face. Banner attempted to console her by resting his head in her lap.

"He's a very evil man. Very evil, and he said someone was going to rescue him soon. I guess they must have come for him because he would have killed us by now, I'm certain of it. I'm so very sorry if I've upset you, sir."

The Captain sat quietly for several minutes before finally speaking.

"Go straight up to your room. After supper, return to your room and lock your door and leave it locked until morning."

Alice rose, her head held low, and slowly took her leave as Banner watched her go, wishing he knew of some way to cheer her. When she was out of his sight, he suddenly froze. Something was not quite right, and he growled. The Captain noticed the change in his behaviour and called him into the cottage.

Back in her room, Alice lay on her bed staring at the

ceiling. As she reviewed all that had transpired since she discovered the plane crash, she gradually convinced herself she had done nothing truly bad, other than disobeying the Captain. She discovered the secret in the forest, she survived, ultimately no one was harmed, and now the danger had passed. Also, she thought, wouldn't the Captain have reacted more angrily if what she had done was really all that wrong? Her spirits were lifted.

After supper, Ridley knocked on the door to the study and entered. Mrs. Thorndike was seated in a corner chair.

"Excuse me, madam," he said as he indicated the telephone on her desk. "Captain Bramwell asked me to place a call on his behalf to Mister Phipps."

"Phipps?" she responded with a frown.

"Yes, madam," Ridley confirmed.

Mrs. Thorndike gestured for him to go ahead and returned to her book.

Donning his reading glasses, Ridley referred to a small notebook he withdrew from his pocket before lifting the receiver and dialing. After a moment, he hung up and dialed again. Not satisfied, he tried rattling the plunger a few times.

Irritated, Mrs. Thorndike asked, "Is there a problem?"

"The telephone doesn't appear to be working, ma'am," he answered.

"I'm not surprised. All of the linemen have gone off to war. We haven't had decent service since the fighting started."

"I shall have to drive into the village in the morning to relay the Captain's message in person."

"What on earth was Phipps doing here so long this afternoon? Didn't the Captain turn him away?"

"Quite the contrary. In fact, he asked Mister Phipps to find his collie in the forest."

"And was he successful?"

"Indeed, yes, ma'am."

"Blast! I was hoping we were rid of the beast. Did Phipps bring back evidence of any boogeyman in the forest?"

"No, ma'am, not to my knowledge. When he left he told me we needn't worry."

"Well, pop into the post office while you're in the village tomorrow and tell them to get our phone line repaired."

Ridley said his good night as he left, and Mrs. Thorndike returned to her book, hopeful that the Captain would finally be finished with all of that "nonsense" about the forest.

Mrs. Belmore finished her chores in the kitchen quite late that evening, making preparations for breakfast to be served the next morning. As was her custom after finishing up her work at night and before preparing for bed, she sat outside the kitchen door and drank a cup of tea and treated herself to a cigarette. When she was done, she went back inside. It wasn't the first time she had neglected to lock the kitchen door behind her.

As for Alice, she had settled into a deep sleep, and was catching up on the rest she had missed during the fitful night before. While she slept, she was unaware of the footsteps in the hall outside.

Mrs. Thorndike tried Alice's door, and after confirming that it was locked, she fished in her pocket for her keychain.

Unlocking the door and pushing it open slightly, she leaned into the room to confirm that Alice was indeed sleeping and then withdrew. She was about to close the door quietly when she stopped and instead left it slightly ajar. It was the way she preferred it to be, just one of many ways she asserted her control. Satisfied, she continued down the hall and downstairs to her bedroom. When she reached her room and turned out her light, the house was dark.

It was not secure.

CHAPTER THIRTEEN

Ridley knocked at the Captain's door much earlier than usual the next morning and was greeted by Banner's bark from inside. Eventually the Captain appeared. He was wearing a robe, and his headscarf had been wrapped hastily. He opened the door slightly as he nudged Banner back to prevent him from escaping.

"Begging your pardon, sir," Ridley said nervously, "I'm sorry to disturb you, but Missus Thorndike thought you should be notified immediately. It's the girl, sir, Miss Alice. She's gone. That is, unless she's here with you."

"Gone?" the Captain asked, blinking his one good eye against the morning light over the butler's shoulder. "Of course she's not here with me. What on earth are you talking about?"

"Well, you see, Anna was the first to notice when she went to the girl's bedroom to fetch her to breakfast. Her bed had been slept in, but she was nowhere to be found. We searched every room in the house, and now we're searching the grounds, but she doesn't seem to be on the property. I wonder, sir, could she have gone into the forest?"

"Not likely. Not without Banner. Uhm … Very well, telephone the Constable and …"

"I'm afraid that's not possible, sir. The telephone hasn't been working all night."

"Good Lord!" the Captain exclaimed. "All right, then look here, I'll get dressed and meet Missus Thorndike at the house. We'll figure out what to do from there. Meanwhile, you are to drive to the village as fast as you can travel. Summon Phipps and the Constable and get them back here along with any other volunteers you find along the way. Tell them we have a drastic emergency here and we need all the help we can get. Go! Hurry!"

Ridley rushed away, and the Captain turned back into the cottage, nearly tripping over Banner, who stood behind him. Reaching the bedroom, he grabbed the pistol he had left on the nightstand and placed it on the bed so that he might reach it quickly, if needed, while he dressed.

When Ridley reached the house, he found Mrs. Thorndike standing on the front steps. Anna and Mrs. Belmore were returning to her after a search of the stables.

"She's not in the stables," Mrs. Belmore gasped as they approached. "We searched it thoroughly."

"Very well," Mrs. Thorndike replied, "The two of you search by the lake again. See if there's anywhere you could have missed. Ridley, check the garage."

"I'm on my way there now, ma'am," he told her. "The Captain is sending me to the village for help. He said he will meet you here momentarily."

Ridley trotted toward the garage, and Mrs. Thorndike felt her body trembling.

"Heaven, help me," she said under her breath. "The Captain will have my hide for certain. Damn the girl! She's done this to get me discharged. I'm sure of it."

She began pacing angrily but was soon interrupted by a shout from Ridley as he came running back from the garage.

"Mrs. Thorndike! Mrs. Belmore! Anna! Come back!" he called out. "She's not here!"

Anna and Mrs. Belmore heard his voice and rushed

back, arriving shortly after Ridley, who stood before Mrs. Thorndike, trying to catch his breath.

"What do you mean?" Mrs. Thorndike asked testily. "How do you know?"

"Because," he panted, "the car has been stolen. The keys are not where I normally hang them, and the car is missing."

"God in heaven!" Mrs. Belmore exclaimed. "Can she even drive?"

"Missus Belmore," he said, clutching his chest. "I don't think you comprehend what's going on here. The girl has been kidnapped. I'm certain of it!"

"Now there'll be hell to pay," Mrs. Thorndike muttered quietly. "Here's the Captain."

Dressing in great haste, he hadn't bothered to put on a tie, and his vest was not buttoned. He was walking rapidly and with great difficulty and nearly fell several times as he approached. Banner was close at his side.

Mrs. Thorndike was the first to speak.

"Captain Bramwell, I assure you I have done all that I could possibly have done to ..."

"Shut up, you stupid woman!" the Captain snarled at her. "Shut up! Wasn't her door lucked last night?"

The expression on her face answered his question. Mrs. Thorndike was about to defend herself when he held his hand up to silence her.

"Listen!" he ordered.

As everyone strained to hear, the Captain turned to Ridley.

"Isn't that a car engine I hear?" he asked the butler, who

was trying very hard to identify a faint sound heard in the distance.

"Why, yes, sir," Ridley confirmed. "I believe it is, and it's coming this way!"

"Oh, thank the Lord," Mrs. Belmore gasped. "Let it be her coming back to us!"

All held their breath until the car was within sight, driving up the road to the house. Their reaction was mixed when it was close enough for them to make out Dr. Finlay behind the wheel. The Captain approached him as he pulled to a stop in the driveway.

"Thank heavens you're here, Doctor," the Captain said to him. "Our car has been stolen, and I must get to the village at once. I'll explain on the way."

The Doctor opened his mouth to speak, but the Captain swiftly opened the rear door to allow Banner to jump in, then he laboriously seated himself in the front passenger seat, pulling his crutch in with him.

"Drive on!" the Captain commanded. "Quickly!"

Doctor Finlay was amazed that his friend, who had practically lived like a hermit for 26 years, was now suddenly rushing toward the center of the local village. He reasoned that it must be for something far more important than a stolen automobile. The Doctor shifted his car in gear and slammed his foot down on the accelerator.

During the drive to the village, the Captain, in fits and starts, related the events that led to Alice's disappearance and the theft of his car.

"I hope I'm not wrong," he said, "but I believe the man we're after is headed in this direction. Alice said he told her he was going to be rescued, and I think it's safe to assume that rescue will be made by air. That means they'll probably attempt a landing on that empty plot of land at the edge of the village."

"Yes," the Doctor agreed, "the military cleared that land not long ago and then abandoned it. Weeds have started to take hold, but I expect it would work sufficiently for a landing, but what makes you think they'll attempt a rescue in broad daylight? Why wouldn't they wait until nightfall?"

"There's a storm expected," the Captain answered, "possibly as early as this evening, and it may last a few days. The Germans may be worried their man will be captured soon. After all, if a little girl and her dog could find him, they may have decided an immediate rescue is worth the risk. He must be a very important man."

"Yes, but what does he want with the girl?" the Doctor wondered.

The Captain gritted his teeth.

"She's his hostage. She'll make good cover while he makes his escape."

Nearing the village, they spotted the Captain's automobile, abandoned on the shoulder of the road.

"Wait here," the Doctor said as he pulled up behind. "Let me give it a once-over."

The Captain waited impatiently. He could feel one of his attacks trying to take hold, and he was doing his very best to keep it at bay. He worried that his resistance was weak, but he fought against it nonetheless as he cursed his own body's weakness. Banner could sense his master's struggle and whined as he leaned forward from the back seat and rested his head on his shoulder.

"I found this," Doctor Finlay said, tossing Alice's blue scarf to the Captain as he returned to the car.

"It's hers," the Captain declared.

"I know," the Doctor agreed as he accelerated suddenly.

At that time of morning there weren't a great many people on the one little road that led through the village. The shopkeepers were greeting one another as they unlocked their doors to prepare for business, and there was a small truck parked in front of a produce merchant delivering goods from a local farm. Nearby, a deliveryman was unloading cans of milk from his horse-drawn wagon, and Phipps, on his way for his morning cup of tea at the small village café, greeted the driver as he passed. He paused by the horse and pulled a partially eaten carrot from his pocket.

"G' mornin' Ethel," he said as he fed the horse. "You be careful you don't work too hard today, right, sweetheart?"

Giving her a pat on the neck, he continued a short distance to his destination. Standing aside, he tipped his cap to the schoolteacher as she exited the café he was about to enter.

"Mornin' Missus Richardson," he greeted her. "Getting an early start on the school day, are we?"

"I thought I'd check on the victory garden the children planted yesterday before I prepare the day's lessons," she answered cheerfully.

"Ah!" He replied. "I wish you good day, then."

He was about to step inside the café when he stopped. He was certain he could hear, very faintly, an airplane engine in the distance. Stepping back into the road, he strained to make out what kind of aircraft might be passing, for the area was not a common route. It took several minutes before the object in the sky was near enough to be seen. As it came nearer, Phipps nearly choked with alarm. He took his L.D.V. position most seriously and had even begun devoting his off-hours studying and memorizing details of enemy aircraft he gleaned from a pamphlet supplied by the Home Guard. Today he was rewarded for his extra effort.

"Good Lord!" he gasped to himself. "It's a bleedin' …"

He pointed to the sky and yelled at the milk deliveryman.

"IT'S A BLEEDIN' IRON ANNIE!"

The milkman looked up in the sky, confused.

"It's a German plane!" Phipps shouted as he ran toward him. "It's loaded with defensive weapons and … Get out of the road! It's an invasion! Everyone get inside!"

The shouting startled the horse, and she attempted to bolt and began rearing as the deliveryman did his best to restrain her. Phipps continued to yell at everyone to stay inside, prompting many to open their doors and step into the road to see what all the fuss was about.

"Here, what's all this?" the thinly built Constable asked as he rushed from his breakfast. His jacket was unbuttoned, and a napkin was still tucked into his collar.

Phipps alerted him to the disaster in the sky, but after studying the plane for a few moments, the Constable shook his head.

"Now why in the name of all that's holy," the Constable began, "would the Jerries want to attack a little, insignificant …"

157

Suddenly a trail of machine gun fire tracked its way along the road as the German aircraft strafed the village on its way over.

Mrs. Richardson had just reached the door of the schoolhouse when she heard the gunfire behind her. Stunned, she hurriedly unlocked the door and rushed inside. In her haste, she hadn't noticed that one of the windows on the side of the building had been jimmied open.

As his car neared the village, Doctor Finlay made a sudden stop.

"Do you hear that?" he asked the Captain.

"It's gunfire!" the Captain responded, and his one good eye began to twitch. Banner, excited and uncertain, barked wildly.

The Doctor accelerated.

"Why would they bother to attack the village?" he asked.

The Captain began shivering as his memory of combat began to engulf him. He wrestled against the demon that was attempting to overtake his nerves.

"Distraction," he stammered, "perhaps a warning to the villagers to stay out of the way, perhaps another stupid young Jerry eager to kill innocent civilians."

The Doctor noticed the Captain's trauma.

"I want you to stay in the car when we arrive," the Doctor told him. "Let me handle this."

"Don't worry about me," the Captain replied with difficulty. "I'll be all right."

Doctor Finlay didn't believe him.

Reaching the village, they found the locals in a state of

pandemonium. Many were gathered in groups while some rushed to check on their neighbors. The Constable was rushing about madly trying to get everyone back inside before the enemy aircraft returned.

The Doctor parked his car and stepped out.

"Thank God!" he heard Phipps call out from across the road. "Over here, Doctor Finlay! Quick!"

Phipps was kneeling at the curb, tending to the milkman, who was bleeding from the shoulder. Mayor Applebee was doing his best to steady the horse. The Doctor reached into the back seat of his car and pushed aside Banner to grab his medical bag before rushing to the injured man.

"Can we move him, Doctor?" Phipps asked. "I fear that aircraft is circling around for another go at it."

The Doctor agreed and called for two stalwart youths standing nearby to assist in moving the injured man into the produce market.

"Have you called for help?" he called over his shoulder as he followed the two men.

"All of our phone lines have been cut," Phipps replied. "Bloody Nazis! I sent a lad over to Steffingshire for help. Pray he makes it through!"

Turning back to the road, Phipps rushed to the produce truck and yelled to the driver, who was attempting, in vain, to start the engine.

"We'll be needin' your truck to move the gun from the square," he told him.

"No use, mate! Those gunshots pierced the engine. This rig ain't goin' nowhere!" the driver replied.

Phipps reacted with frustration, then raced toward Mayor Applebee, who was still struggling with the mare.

"Here!" Phipps yelled, "Ethel can help us move the field artillery from the square. I'll try to shoot the Junker out o' the sky, if I can."

"That old cannon?" the Mayor asked incredulously. "It'll blow up in your face 'afore it'll shoot down any Nazis, even if you did have any ammunition for it!"

"I've got two shells," Phipps countered as he grabbed the horse's reins from him. "That's two chances we don't otherwise possess. We got to give it a try. Come on!"

Spying the Constable nearby, he called for his assistance.

"Lend a hand!" he said quickly. "Help me get Ethel unhitched, but keep her in harness. We'll use her to pull the gun. Hurry it along!"

Captain Bramwell, meanwhile, was standing beside the car. Banner had jumped from the back seat to the front and pushed his way out through the open door to stand beside him. It was the first time the collie had left the estate, and he stood nervously beside his master, shivering slightly, while the Captain grasped his crutch firmly, observing the chaos in the road.

Banner brought the Captain to his senses. Looking up at him, he barked once as if to ask what they were doing there.

"Yes, of course!" the Captain declared and reached inside the car to retrieve Alice's blue scarf. Now the mental trauma he had been experiencing left him as he became obsessed with his mission to find her. He gathered the cloth into a ball and held it before Banner's face.

"It's hers, boy!" he said. "Find her. Find Alice. Find

her!"

Banner sniffed the scarf thoroughly, moving his nose around one side of the object, then around the other. When he had fully recognized the smell, he turned away from the Captain and looked about before lowering his head to the ground and moving about in circles, stopping occasionally, retracing the areas he had already explored, gradually moving in one direction. He stopped at one point and looked back at the Captain, who was following him as he slowly travelled down the road. He wasn't finding a trail to Alice.

"Go on!" the Captain encouraged him. "Find her, boy. Hurry!"

Banner turned and began sniffing the air, gradually lifting his head higher and aiming his nose in different directions before him. Suddenly he stopped moving his head and concentrated in one direction down the road. He had picked up a scent cone that was being lightly blown in his direction. He looked back and barked the news to the Captain, then began running toward the source of the smell.

The Captain turned to call for Doctor Finlay, but he was not in earshot as he tended to the wounded man in the market nearby. Gathering his strength, the Captain attempted to follow Banner.

Once more the German aircraft flew low over the village and delivered a shower of gunfire down the street as it passed. The Captain stepped into an alley to conceal himself, then leaned out in time to witness a barrage of bullets hitting the ground as they made their way directly toward Banner. The dog noticed the trail of gunfire heading his way and dashed out of the pathway just before it reached him, barely avoiding a direct hit but still close enough that dust and debris thrown up by the bullets striking the ground flew into his eyes as the machine gun fire continued down the road.

Banner squinted, shook his head and rubbed at his eyes with his paw as the Captain approached him. When he was almost beside him, the dog shook his head again and blinking heavily, continued on his mission.

At the edge of the village, the collie stopped and stood frozen. He was looking toward the schoolhouse that sat beside the open field. The Captain observed Banner's attention and called him back to where he stood by a grain supply that marked the beginning of the village proper. He moved behind several sacks filled with provisions that were stacked just high enough to provide concealment and attempted to silence his dog, who returned to him, whining excitedly. Soon Banner's whine turned into a low growl. He had detected another scent on Alice's scarf, one that he hated, and it was emanating from the building across the road. The Captain withdrew his pistol from his pocket and tried to make out, with his one eye, what lay behind the schoolhouse window.

Inside the small schoolroom, Major Richter leaned against the wall and peered into the sky through a window that faced the open field. He was wearing a torn uniform jacket, and he kept the pistol he held in his hand trained on Alice and Mrs. Richardson, who sat on the floor embracing one another before the teacher's desk nearby.

"Yes," he said, glancing at his wristwatch, "everything according to plan. In moments my rescuers will land, and I will be away from here."

He looked back at his two captives.

"But I won't be alone."

Moving from the window, he leaned toward them.

"My dear Missus Schoolteacher, if only you hadn't chosen today to report to your classroom earlier than normal. For that, you shall accompany the girl and me on a little trip to my homeland, where the two of you will be privileged to participate in a program I shall recommend to the Fuehrer himself. It is a program that will greatly demoralize the stupid British civilians."

"Wasn't that the purpose of the Blitz, to demoralize us?" Mrs. Richardson asked.

"Partially, perhaps," he replied, "but I'm afraid our strategic bombing missions haven't quite worked out as well in that regard as the Wehrmacht might have hoped. The plan I will recommend will surely be more successful. When the people of Great Britain learn of the capture of a schoolteacher and a young girl from a small, insignificant little village right under their very noses and when they see newsreel footage and newspaper articles showing the two of you living under armed guard in a German concentration camp, their confidence will surely be shaken. They will begin to doubt their own security and the safety of their own women and children. 'How could the great British army fail to keep such a thing from happening?' they will ask."

Alice embraced Mrs. Richardson and hugged tightly.

"And then," he continued, "when the remarkable weapon I am developing is introduced to the world shortly thereafter, Great Britain and all its allies will realize the hopelessness of their resistance."

"You are wrong, sir," Mrs. Richardson interrupted. "Our kidnapping will not demoralize our countrymen. It will only incite them to fight harder. What will you do with us when that happens?"

"Some people die in our concentration camps," Richter replied with a shrug. "It happens."

Down the road in the village square, Phipps and his impromptu volunteers were improvising a rigging out of Ethel's harness that would allow them to pull the old World War I weapon to the open area at the edge of the village near the schoolhouse. From there, Phipps hoped to have a clear shot at the aircraft when it returned to fire at them.

Ethel, however, was being uncooperative. The gunfire had unnerved her, and she resisted every effort the men put forth to keep her under control while they hooked her up to the cannon.

"Come on, Ethel, me ol' girl," Phipps said to her as he held her head to his chest. "Ain't I been a good friend to you all these years, carrots every mornin' and all? Show a little gratitude to your old Phipps, what say?"

The mare nudged him aside and shook her head as if to say, "Let's get on with it, then," and Phipps pulled at her bridle as the Mayor and Constable pushed the weapon behind her.

A 15-year-old girl burst from the café and attempted to assist them.

"No, Millie!" Phipps yelled to her. "I need you to run to my workshop and fetch the two artillery shells stored in the corner near the back. They're sitting in a little wagon and they're covered with a canvas tarp. You'll find the door unlocked. Meet us by the schoolhouse and hurry! We haven't a moment to lose. And BE CAREFUL!"

Elsewhere, Captain Bramwell was trying to steady the hand that held his pistol. He laid his one good arm on top of a seed bag stacked before him and did his best to focus his one good eye on the gunsight, aiming it toward the door. He hadn't fired the weapon since he was wounded, and with his several impairments, he lacked the ability and confidence to fire a shot accurately. Nevertheless, he had no one else to help. No one else but Banner.

The collie stood at his side, shivering with anticipation, waiting for one word, one signal giving him permission to rush to the little girl to whom he had become so attached. He was wildly torn between obeying his master and running to rescue her from the man he knew instinctively was intent on doing her harm. Did his master understand as well as he the danger she was in and how there wasn't a moment to lose? Banner was but a hairsbreadth away from disobeying his command. It could happen any second.

"Steady, Banner," the Captain gently commanded him as he kept his eye on his gunsight. "Steady, old boy!"

Back at the schoolhouse window, Richter could hear the drone of the airplane engine as it approached again, and he saw its approach, flying low.

"I've got to signal them," he said, hastily turning toward his two prisoners. "They have to know I am here and I am ready."

He grabbed Mrs. Richardson and held her closely in front of him with one arm while he held his gun to her head.

"You will serve as my shield until we reach the aircraft,"

he said and then nodded toward Alice. "You will walk before me and lead the way, but stay close. If you try to run away, the teacher will die, do you understand?"

Alice nodded. She resisted the urge to cry. She knew this was a time she must not show weakness, and she would not humiliate herself before her enemy.

"Now, go ahead," he told her. "Go quickly. Out the front door and then turn immediately toward the field. We must signal the aircraft we are ready so he will land and pick us up. Go!"

Alice looked into Mrs. Richardson's face. She was trembling as she cried.

"You needn't worry, ma'am," Alice assured her. "We'll be all right."

"Shut up and go!" Richter shouted. "We don't have time for such nonsense! Open the door!"

She calmly turned to face him.

"I feel very sorry for you," she said to him. "You don't have a dog. I do."

Richter prepared to shout at her again, but she coolly turned and led the way to the door.

The Captain froze as he saw the schoolhouse door open. He watched as Alice stepped out confidently and turned toward the field, closely followed by Major Richter and his captive. The German kept his eyes trained on the girl and didn't notice that he was being watched from across the road.

Now Banner was unsure what to do. Alice was walking ahead. She didn't seem to be afraid. Was his urge to disobey the Captain and run to her the right action to take? For the moment, he trusted his master's wisdom. After all, the Captain could see her too, but Banner would not stay put for long. Of that, the collie was certain.

Captain Bramwell cursed himself for his inability to act. If he fired and missed, the German might pull the trigger on the woman he was holding as his shield.

Then, as he watched them walking, something stirred deep inside him, and in an instant, he recognized who the woman was. He hadn't thought he could face any more pressure than he was already feeling as he watched Alice, but now that he recognized the other victim, the crisis took on an additional strain. It was unbearable.

Banner recognized the Captain's tension and he sensed that he may have to take command. His master was no longer in condition to do what must be done. Banner would do it.

Behind him, the Captain could hear Phipps and his crew as they pulled up with the 18-pounder and began making preparations to commence firing on the enemy aircraft which at that moment was flying low, surveying the area. Molly rushed up to them, pulling the wagon and two artillery shells.

The group on the field had reached a point 13 yards out when Major Richter ordered Alice to halt and begin waving her arms to signal the pilot. She reluctantly obeyed, raising her arms outright at chest level and slowly swinging them back and forth.

"Higher and faster!" Richter yelled at her as he manipulated a bullet into the chamber of the gun he was holding at Mrs. Richardson's head. Alice complied.

The pilot in the plane waved back and ascended slightly, heading out to a distance where he could turn and allow plenty of room for a landing. As the aircraft passed, Alice shuddered as she noticed a man aboard seated behind a machine gun that was pointed directly at her.

Banner tensed. The man with Alice had yelled at her angrily, and she was waving her arms. Was it a signal that she needed help? The collie was through trying to figure it all out, and he broke from behind the pile of bags where he had been hiding and rushed toward his girl with the speed of lightning.

"Banner, no!" the Captain yelled after him.

Richter heard the command and turned his head to see the beast, his veins filled with fire, headed directly toward him. The snarl on the dog's face left no doubt as to his intentions.

Alice saw Banner too, and her heart nearly stopped.

"Banner, no!" she cried. "Go back! Go back!"

It was too late. The collie was not to be stopped. He had waited too long for this.

Major Richter was delighted with this opportunity, and he smiled as he aimed his gun directly at Banner. He fired once, but at that moment Mrs. Richardson struggled against him, causing him to very narrowly miss the dog. Cursing, he prepared to fire again.

The events that followed all occurred in a matter of seconds.

With the German's gun pointed away from his captive, the Captain seized the opportunity to take action, and with a prayer on his lips, he took careful aim and pulled the trigger of his weapon. His bullet struck mid-shoulder, which caused Richter's arm to recoil and lose the grip on his pistol, which went flying out of his reach onto the field as he fell to one knee, clutching his arm in pain. His grip released, Mrs. Richardson swiftly turned and ran from the field, passing Banner along the way.

The Captain thrust his gun into his jacket pocket and hobbled after Banner, while Phipps readied his artillery for firing.

Confused, Alice turned to Richter. Unable to use his right arm and unable to retrieve his gun, he reached behind his back with his left arm and withdrew his dagger and staggered to his feet, preparing to meet the attack of the dog who was nearly on top of him.

Quickly summing up the situation, Alice jumped in front of Banner to prevent him from attacking Richter, who would undoubtedly have impaled him with his dagger, but the dog had been running with such speed that he smashed into her. The momentum knocked her off her feet. Managing to place herself between Banner and his objective, she clutched the ruff around his neck and did her best to hold him tight, wrestling with him as he attempted to break loose from her grip.

At that moment, the German aircraft was preparing to land on the field, and with landing gear set, it was prepared to touch down. Before the pilot could complete his landing, however, he was met with the explosion of an artillery shell that struck the field directly in front of the plane. Instinctively, the pilot pulled the aircraft up.

Seeing the failed landing, Richter began yelling.

"No! No! Come back!" He cried. *"Du cannst mich nicht verlassen!"*

As the plane lifted, Phipps yelled orders to his helpers as

they rushed about madly, attempting to reload their weapon.

"Quick! Quick!" he screamed. "We almost got him. Hurry! It's getting away!"

Faster than could be expected from such an inexperienced crew, the M1 was reloaded and ready to fire. Looking through the single eyepiece mounted at the back of the weapon, he turned the crank for elevation and then another for direction and as soon as he had the target in his sight, he stepped back, clutched the firing lever and pulled.

After the shell was fired, there was a brief second of silence as the shot made its way to its destination. In an instant, the round struck its target, blowing off a wing and sending the plane instantly smashing to the ground. There was a tremendous explosion, and the hull of the plane burst into flame. Phipps and his men cheered and began dancing with Molly.

Richter stood, deflated, tears streaming as he watched his hope for rescue go up in flames. After a moment, he turned, seething.

"Damn you, you stupid girl!" he screamed with a crazed, animalistic growl. *"Ich wirst jetzt sterben!"*

He raised the dagger above his head, preparing a death thrust into Alice. As he held his arm high, the sleeve of his shirt and jacket pulled back just far enough to reveal his soft, white wrist. Banner had marked that tempting morsel that day they met in the woods, and he had so wanted to grasp it in his teeth then. Now there was nothing to stop him and before Richter could react, Banner furiously leaped at him with the speed of a rocket and grabbed his target exactly where he had intended, easily sinking his teeth into that tender skin and grasping the bone beneath. The German dropped his weapon and fell backward to the ground, screaming and flailing as Banner held his arm in a vice-like grip.

Alice stepped back, unsure what to do as Captain Bramwell finally reached her side. They were immediately joined by the Mayor, the Constable and Phipps, who was carrying his rifle.

Banner was still clutching Major Richter's wrist and had begun tearing at it as if the limb itself was a creature that had to be destroyed. Richter was unable to put up much resistance, as his other arm had been incapacitated by the gunshot wound. He pleaded for the onlookers to call the dog off.

"Banner!" the Captain called out. "Banner! Release! Let him go!"

The dog did not respond.

Alice leaned in to him and tried to pull him away.

"That's enough! Banner, that's enough, boy!" she said to him gently, and he gradually pulled back, growling and snarling as Richter tried to move away.

"That'll do right there," Phipps said, aiming his rifle at his head. "You'll be serving out the rest of your life in one of His Majesty's prisoner-of-war camps, I expect."

Richter tried to clutch the arm bleeding from the dog bite with the hand of the arm that had been shot.

"Help me! Help me!" He pleaded. "Can't you see I'm bleeding to death?"

"I'm sure the doctor will be here with all haste," Phipps assured him with fake sympathy. "You just be patient now.

Blimey! That's a nasty looking dog bite you got there. Might've even pierced a major blood vessel. That hurt? 'Cause it looks like it hurts real bad."

Turning to look at Banner, whom Alice was still holding back, Phipps asked the dog, "Did you deliver that wound? Nice work, Private Banner. You'll get a promotion for this for sure."

Snapping to attention, Phipps delivered a snappy salute to him.

"Carry on, old boy!" he said.

Several military vehicles turned onto the field and approached.

"Well, there they are!" Phipps declared. "Just in time to save the day!"

Having calmed Banner, Alice rose and rushed to Captain Bramwell. She threw her arms around him.

"It's Banner you must thank," he said, his voice choking.

Reaching into his pocket, he withdrew Alice's scarf and draped it tenderly around her shoulders.

"Come. Let's leave this place," he said.

Arm in arm, they walked from the field while she held her free hand steadily on Banner's back. When they had reached the edge of the field, they were met by Doctor Finlay, who was rushing toward the injured man.

"Is everyone all right here?" he asked.

"Everyone but the German," the Captain replied. "You needn't rush."

"Ah!" the Doctor responded as he saw where the men had gathered around the fallen Nazi. "Oh, listen, you'll have to make your own way back to the estate, I'm afraid. I need to check back on my other patient after I take care of this one. Do you think you can manage a lift back?"

"I'll be pleased to drive Captain Bramwell home," Mrs. Richardson volunteered from nearby.

The Captain looked at her with surprise, and for a moment they stared at each other.

"Won't you come with me, Alice?" she said, holding out a hand to her. "We'll fetch my car and drive back 'round here to pick up the Captain."

Alice obliged, and Banner accompanied the two of them as they walked away.

"Very good, then," the Doctor said looking after them, then started off. Stopping, he turned back to the Captain. "Oh, by the way, I'll drop in on you later this evening. I have news of Alice's father."

Before the Captain could respond, Doctor Finlay hastened away.

CHAPTER FOURTEEN

The events of the past several hours had left Alice drained, and as Mrs. Richardson's car hummed along the road leading back to the estate, she rested her head on Banner, who lay next to her on the back seat, and was soon lulled to sleep. Having her and the Captain safe and near comforted the collie, and as they travelled, relaxed and content, he, too, became quite drowsy. Though he struggled to hold his head upright, he soon yielded to the pull of slumber and gently laying his head down next to Alice, he breathed a heavy sigh and joined her in an untroubled sleep.

For most of the ride, the two adults were silent. As they neared the front gate of the estate, the Captain looked at the two sleeping passengers in the back seat, and Mrs. Richardson finally spoke.

"Your collie is a hero, isn't he?" she asked. "I shouldn't be surprised if he were presented a medal for his bravery."

"There will be no such foolishness," the Captain replied. "Do you think such a thing would mean anything to him? All he asks is a friendly pat on the head and a bit of extra food in his bowl. That would mean as much as much to him as any ridiculous medal."

They continued in silence a while longer until they passed through the gate.

"You left her out there," the Captain said to her, staring straight ahead. "When you were able to escape, you ran and left her on the field. Didn't you?"

"I … yes, I suppose I did, didn't I?" Mrs. Richardson stammered. She hadn't thought about it. She stopped the car.

"I'm sorry," she said as she started to cry. "I'm so

terribly sorry. I'm not brave. I left her and I left you. It seems to be a weakness of mine, doesn't it? When things become too difficult, I run away."

There was a period of silence before he asked, "Are you happy, Helen?"

"I suppose so," she said, fishing for a handkerchief in her purse. "Not completely. I can't forget the past. I can't help thinking how very much I loved you and how lonely you must be."

"You needn't worry then. I live my life with a collie who will not allow me to be lonely. He loves me absolutely, and he forgives me for transgressions I haven't even yet committed. As for the past, I have decided I'll let it remain the past. All of it. At least, as much as I can with my physical limitations. I'm going to try, anyway."

"Now, he said, nodding toward the house, "please continue."

Dabbing at the tears on her cheek, Mrs. Richardson continued onward, stopping at the front doorstep of the estate. Ridley had seen the car approaching and was there to open the door for the Captain. Mrs. Thorndike joined him.

Banner and Alice were wakened by the opening of the front car door. Alice opened her door, and Banner eagerly jumped out, barking merrily. As she stepped out, he ran circles around her, and she laughed.

With Ridley's help, the Captain stood. Leaning back into the car he nodded toward Alice and Banner.

"You see that?" he said to Mrs. Richardson. "Looking at them now, who could imagine what they were forced to endure just a short while ago? Let the past go, Helen, and you will find true happiness."

His words did not stop her tears, which continued to flow long after Ridley had closed the car door and she had driven away.

Captain Bramwell watched Alice and Banner play for several minutes.

"Is everything all right, sir?" Ridley finally asked. "Would you care for some tea and sandwiches at the cottage?"

"Everything is fine, Ridley," the Captain answered. "Miss Piper will join me. Also, bring along some of that marvelous cake Missus Belmore served at lunch yesterday, if she has any left."

He gestured for Mrs. Thorndike to join them.

"Now listen," he said. "You are to instruct Anna to prepare my old room upstairs. I shall sleep there tomorrow evening, and day after tomorrow we shall begin moving all of my things out of the cottage and back into the house. Missus Thorndike, I would like to review the books tomorrow afternoon and when we have finished, you shall no longer be required to serve as manager of my estate. I shall be assuming those duties myself. You will be returning to your original duties as housekeeper. I will resume my responsibilities as head of this estate, and I shall be taking up residence in the house, where I belong."

"Yes, sir," Ridley said with a broad smile as he turned to arrange lunch. Mrs. Thorndike, solemn as ever, nodded and returned to the house as Captain Bramwell stood watching Banner and Alice play.

Alice returned to her room and collapsed on the bed, thoroughly exhausted, and slept through the light lunch the

Captain had ordered.

Banner remained close by Alice's side throughout the rest of the day and even at that evening's supper, which was served to Alice in the main dining room. Mrs. Thorndike ate her meal with the rest of the staff in the kitchen so she was not present to raise any fuss about the dog's presence. After supper, Ridley informed Alice that The Captain had summoned her to join him and Doctor Finlay in the study.

Alice found it strange to find the Captain seated behind the desk in place of Mrs. Thorndike, and she was greeted warmly by the Doctor, who invited her to sit next to him in front.

"I see our hero has not left your side," he said, noticing Banner.

"He hasn't let me out of his sight since this morning," she replied, and the dog replied by resting his head in her lap while she stroked his fur.

"I have some very wonderful news for you, Alice," he began. "Your father has come home."

"What?" Alice asked, stunned. "Is he all right? Why was he sent home?"

"Well," the Doctor replied, "he has been wounded, but do not worry. He's under my care, and I'm pleased to inform you he will be well enough to leave the hospital in a day or so."

Alice began to cry. "He was wounded? How badly?"

"Now you needn't worry. It's not serious. He took some enemy fire in the leg, but he's going to be fine. He may have to use a cane to get about, and I'm afraid he's been deemed unfit for further military duties, but he's going to be fine. You can trust me."

Alice leaped up and began pacing about, talking quickly.

"Oh, my goodness!" she exclaimed excitedly, "He's home? Now? When can I see him?"

"Tomorrow morning, bright and early. I shall return to pick you up, and we'll drive from here straight to the hospital. You're going home. How will that suit you?"

"But … where shall we live? Our home was destroyed. What shall we do?"

"That, my dear, is another bit of exciting news. I'm told you have an Uncle Paul who lives in the United States. California, I believe. He has a dairy there, and he and your father are going to go into business together. You and your father will live with your uncle and his family and your father on a farm, where I'm told there are lots of animals. How will that suit you?"

"Did you hear that, Banner?" she asked, turning to him excitedly. "Only …"

Suddenly realizing what the news meant, she looked at Captain Bramwell, but he was looking down at his desk.

"Yes," the Doctor said, with understanding, "Banner must remain behind, I'm afraid. You must remember, he came here to help Captain Bramwell. He's his dog, my dear."

Alice dropped to her knees next to Banner and gazed into his eyes as she scratched him behind his ear, and the tears began to flow.

"How could such good news be so bad?" she asked, then suddenly stood and ran from the room. Banner tried to follow, but she had left him behind, and he began whining and scratching at the door she had closed as she departed.

Alice spent the rest of the evening, lying on her bed crying endlessly into her pillow. Mrs. Thorndike entered her room at bedtime and silently packed her suitcase as Alice changed into her nightgown.

"There," Mrs. Thorndike said when she had finished. She avoided looking at the girl directly. "Now you'll be ready for the Doctor when he returns tomorrow morning. I left your new church clothes out for you to wear. You'll want to look your best when you see your father."

She stopped at the door and waited until Alice had settled into her bed.

"Goodnight, Miss Piper," the housekeeper said and turned out the light. As usual, when she left, she carefully left the door slightly ajar.

Torn between the joy of reuniting with her father and the pain of leaving behind forever the only thing in the world she loved nearly as much as he, Alice found sleep impossible. Her memory of all she had experienced in the previous few days was completely dominated by thoughts of the collie.

After nearly two hours had passed, Alice, still consumed with exhaustion, was finally on the verge of sleep. She didn't notice the door to her room as it was nudged open slightly, nor did she notice the cricket ball that was gently dropped through the gap, bouncing once before it rolled across the floor, eventually coming to rest midway between the doorway and her bed.

Beyond the entrance, Alice's visitor waited for an invitation to enter. When none was forthcoming, he slowly peeked around the door. Finding her unresponsive, he lightly crossed the floor, picking up the ball before carefully dropping it on the bed beside its sleeping occupant, who lay facing the opposite direction, her face buried in her pillow. He placed his paw beside the ball and waited.

After a few moments, Alice was startled awake when she sensed she was not alone, and she turned to see Banner watching her, his head tilted slightly as if inviting her to play. Having been noticed, he pushed the ball toward her with his nose.

Alice embraced him, and he jumped onto the bed and snuggled while outside, a soothing rain had begun to fall. The girl and the dog remained in that position the rest of the night.

The next morning, Banner at her side, and with the rain having subsided, Alice walked the familiar path to the Captain's cottage for the last time. Rounding the corner at the back of the building, she found Ridley serving breakfast. To her surprise, there was a setting for two. The butler looked up from the table and smiled, almost imperceptibly, before departing.

Banner rushed to his master's side, and the Captain reached down with his good hand and touched his head. Alice was not prepared for her second surprise of the morning, and her jaw dropped, not with amazement at what she saw, but because it was so unexpected.

He was standing in his customary spot, looking toward the forest, his back toward Alice. He wasn't wearing his scarf.

"Captain Bramwell?" she asked uneasily.

Gradually he turned to face her, allowing Alice time to prepare for what she was about to see.

His face was not recognizable as a face at all. His skin, beginning with the top of his head and extending below his neck into his open collar, was completely covered in terrible burn scars, leaving only a few traces of scraggly hair atop his skull. His right eye was missing below a brow that was badly deformed and swollen and protruded hideously outward, while his left eye was cloudy and bulged slightly out of its socket. As Alice imagined, there were no ears on his head and in place of his nose there was only a gap such as one would see on a Halloween skeleton's face. There were no lips on his mouth, and skin sealed one side shut, while the other side remained open, revealing a mouth containing only a smattering of cracked and discolored teeth, over which lay a mangled tongue.

Though Alice was surprised, she was not shocked or disgusted at what she saw, nor was she inclined to feel condescendingly sympathetic. In fact, she found herself strangely calm. The Captain, with Banner's help, had become her friend during the last few days, and this sudden display of trust on his part made her admire and respect him even more. She was deeply touched.

"I should have warned you, I suppose," he said to her after she had been given enough time to absorb the vision standing before her. "But the more I thought about it, the more I realised that if you were really the person I believe you to be, and if you are truly my friend, you would be no more repulsed than Banner is.

"You have been naturally curious, and you deserve to see me as I am. I hope that what you see before you is not some monster, but a man."

Alice approached him, taking his injured hand and leading him to the table, where she withdrew a chair and looked up into his face with a smile.

They enjoyed their breakfast together, and though the Captain consumed his food with difficulty, he was not embarrassed to eat in front of Alice.

When they had finished, they shared a pot of tea and he became strangely silent.

"Is something bothering you, sir?" she asked.

"I think we're going to get more of that rain this morning that the forecasters promised," he observed, ignoring her question.

Alice noticed his attempt to brighten the moment, but before she could question him, Ridley returned.

"The Doctor has arrived, sir," the butler announced.

"Ask him to wait, please," the Captain instructed. "We'll be along shortly."

"I had best be going," Alice said, rising from her chair.

"Wait," he said, struggling to his feet. "You're forgetting something, I believe. Or perhaps I should say you are forgetting some*one*."

She thought she had misunderstood what he was saying, and she refused to allow herself to believe what she at first thought he meant. She did not want to be disappointed. It would be too much to bear.

"What do you mean?" she asked nervously.

"Your best friend, of course," he said, and looked down at Banner, who was standing next to him. He nudged the collie forward, and he joined Alice.

Once again, Alice felt as if her heart were being torn apart.

"But you can't give him up!" she said, crying again. "He means too much to you. He's your very best friend. You need him!"

"He's your best friend as well," the Captain said. His voice was not strong, and he spoke with considerable difficulty. "And since he would not be able to choose between us, I have chosen for him. Yes, I have needed him, but he has given me what I need, and now it's time for all of us to move on. I have made my decision. Now, hurry along. You mustn't keep the Doctor waiting."

Alice hesitated.

"Go, I say!" the Captain said to her, his impatience growing. "Please. I feel one of my spells coming on, and I want our parting to be a pleasant one. You know how I am when I lose my temper. Don't ruin our last goodbye."

"Thank you," was all she managed to say as she turned away from him. She knew there was nothing more she could say.

As Banner walked beside her, he didn't pause to look back. He didn't know he was leaving forever, though he sensed something strange was about to take place.

When Alice and Banner were gone, Captain Bramwell remained.

"Thank you," he said to himself. Like Alice, it was all that was left to be said, and he meant it for the collie.

For the first time since he had been injured, he cried.

At the front of the house, Alice found Doctor Finlay

standing beside his car, holding the front door open. Ridley was placing her suitcase into the boot. Mrs. Thorndike and the staff were lined up in front of the house to bid her goodbye.

She stood before the Doctor, wishing he could make a difficult decision for her.

"Captain Bramwell informed me about his farewell gift to you," he said. "I know what Banner meant to him. This is probably the greatest gift anyone will ever give you."

She nodded, unable to speak, then turned and walked to the line of servants to say goodbye. She thanked Ridley for looking after the Captain, she thanked Anna for covering for her when she snuck back into the house, her clothes a mess, and she told Mrs. Belmore that she would pray for her son's safe return. Mrs. Thorndike was last in line, and she was looking down, her face a blank.

"You mustn't forget this," she said, emotionless. Reaching into her pocket, she withdrew Banner's cricket ball.

"Anna found it when she was cleaning this morning," she said, handing it to Alice. "I'm sure the dog wouldn't want to be without it. Good luck to you, Miss."

"Thank you, Missus Thorndike," she said as she turned to go. Alice knew it was the most she could hope for from her, and she also knew how difficult it must have been.

Banner was waiting for Alice at the car door.

"I think a seasoned war hero like Banner has earned the right to sit up front with us, wouldn't you agree?" the Doctor asked.

Alice nodded and gestured for the collie to jump inside. He complied, and as she prepared to seat herself next to him, she noticed that the Captain stood watching from the head of the trail that led back to the cottage. It was the same spot she had first seen Banner. He looked old and weak, and though his broken face was incapable of reflecting any emotion, he looked sad.

The Doctor started his car and drove away, while everyone who had come to see her off waved goodbye. When the car had left, Captain Bramwell turned and hobbled back toward his cottage.

As they neared the gate, Banner became upset and kept nervously looking back toward the house. Alice started to calm him, but then stopped.

The collie jumped over the front seat into the back. One of the rear door windows remained open, and he stuck his head out, barking back in the direction of the house.

Alice tried to ignore him at first, and then loudly commanded the Doctor to stop the car.

He watched her as she got out of the car and opened the back door. Banner anxiously jumped out and started to run back toward the house before stopping and running back to Alice where he barked frantically, and repeatedly started to run back to the house and then back to Alice again.

"He doesn't understand," the Doctor said. "He wants you both and he can only have one."

With all the strength she could muster, Alice pointed toward the house.

"Go!" she commanded, and at first Banner complied until he realised she would not be going with him, and he returned.

Alice threw Banner his cricket ball and once again

insisted, "Go!"

Banner ran to fetch the ball, but when he saw Alice starting to get back into the car, he dropped it and returned. When Alice saw that he was on his way back, she quickly looked about her, and locating a dirt clod, she threw it, barely missing him, and he stopped and looked at her, trying hard to understand.

"Go away, you stupid dog! I never want to see you again!" she screamed, tears streaming down her face. She grabbed two more dirt clods and threw them at him. One of them grazed him, but he remained still. He had stopped moving and he had stopped barking. Now he understood, and Alice could tell that his heart was breaking.

Reaching an impasse, Alice stopped throwing dirt clods, and for a moment the two stood looking at one other for the last time.

"I love you so much," she said softly through her tears. "Never forget that."

Then she got back in the car, and the Doctor drove away as rain again began to fall.

Banner watched the car go but remained where he stood for several minutes, allowing the raindrops to dampen his fur, before turning to walk slowly back toward the house, his tail low.

Doctor Finlay said nothing, but shortly after they had left the estate, he reached over the back seat and retrieved an item that he handed to Alice. It was the blue scarf her mother had given her. She held it close to her face all the way to Canterbury.

www.ingramcontent.com/pod-product-compliance
Lightning Source LLC
Chambersburg PA
CBHW070303120726
47910CB00007B/2360